Greylad[illegible]

MURDE[illegible]

Josephine Mary Wedde[illegible]ompson was born in April 1924, the [illegible] four children of a school-master badly wound[illegible] in the First World War and the novelist Joanna Cannan. Like many women before her, Miss Cannan had turned to writing to support her family; as well as writing detective stories and literary novels, she single-handedly created the 'pony book', a new genre which inspired her three daughters, Josephine, Christine and Diana, to emulate and make their own. All three sisters were expert horsewomen and ran their own Grove Riding School near Henley-on-Thames. When Josephine's early ambition to become a vet was thwarted by an unconventional and rather haphazard education, she turned to writing with her first books being published in 1946. Over the next 50 years she wrote over thirty more pony books, a handful of non-fiction equestrian titles, and three novels for adults; the murder mysteries *Gin and Murder* (1959), *They Died in the Spring* (1960) and *Murder Strikes Pink* (1963). She had long involvement with the British branch of International PEN, which campaigns for writers' freedom in authoritarian regimes, and was awarded the MBE in 1984 for services to literature. Josephine Pullein-Thompson died in June 2014, aged 90.

BY THE SAME AUTHOR

Gin and Murder
They Died in the Spring

Over 30 pony books for children

MURDER STRIKES PINK

JOSEPHINE PULLEIN-THOMPSON

Greyladies

Published by
Greyladies
an imprint of The Old Children's Bookshelf

ISBN 978-1-907503-39-9

Set in Sylfaen / Perpetua
Printed and bound in the UK by Charlesworth Press
Wakefield

MURDER STRIKES PINK

CHAPTER ONE

IT WAS FOUR O'CLOCK and the heat of the day was still unabated. In the ring, a desert of friable dun-coloured grass, save for the rich dark patches of peat spread before and after each gaily painted fence, there was no escape from the sun; since early morning it had burned down with unremitting fierceness, reducing the judges, the competitors and the horses to a limp and irritable exhaustion. In the enclosure what shade there was, cast by the white bulk of the refreshment tent, had been sought avidly by the wilting spectators. All through the long hot day they had jostled their deck chairs contentiously, for keeping a place in this dark oasis of shade, as the sun moved round, had become far more important to most of them than anything which went on in the ring.

Theodora Thistleton had remained comparatively unaffected by the heat, but she was infuriated by the poor performances of her horses and the secretaries, recognising the signs of rising anger, sat one on either side of her in uneasy silence. As the prize winners, rosetted and applauded, cantered from the ring, Molly Steer, her nervousness increased by the knowledge that her deodorant had ceased to be effective, blundered into speech.

'Oh, the sound of those poor animals' hooves on that ground; the jar must be dreadful—'

'Hoofs,' snapped Theodora Thistleton, 'and if either of

you mention the state of the ground again I shall go mad.'

'Oh, I *am* sorry, Miss Thistleton.' Molly Steer's large, anxious face flushed red and her pale weak eyes blinked behind the green diamante-decorated spectacles. So unkind, she thought. Joy does nothing to help; we just sit and sit in this dreadful uncomfortable silence. But Theodora Thistleton was already getting to her feet and straightening her tall gaunt figure, clothed in a depressing dress of brown silk, vaguely patterned with green leaves. A beige chiffon scarf tried, vainly, to conceal the long scraggy neck and a brown pudding basin of a straw hat topped the severe and elongated face with its huge tombstone teeth and angry grey-green eyes. Behind her back the secretaries mouthed at each other. 'It's not my turn,' hissed Molly Steer, 'I went with her last time,' and she tried to look as though she intended to stay firmly in her seat, but Joy Hemming, fair, faded and starveling, merely mouthed back, 'Not me,' and sat tight.

Theodora Thistleton was already threading her way through the deck chairs; at any moment she would realise that she was unaccompanied. As usual, Molly Steer gave way first; blinking, swallowing and stumbling over the rows of feet, she followed her employer.

It was typical of Theodora Thistleton's attitude towards her staff that she let the plump, sweating and obviously suffering Molly follow her across the show-ground and then, when she reached the first row of horseboxes, she turned and said, 'I shan't want you; I'm going to have a few words with Christina; you'd better go back.'

'Yes, Miss Thistleton,' Molly answered meekly, but her heart raged. So unkind, thought her mind, limited by its meagre vocabulary, but her heart raged without the need to transform emotion to words. And then, an unaccustomed feeling of mutiny sweeping over her, she sat down on the grass and took off her shoes.

Christina Scott knew what to expect. For seven shows in a row she had failed to win T.T. a rosette and everyone, she reflected, knew what the old money-bag was like over winning; she had to have her bit of ribbon—or else. After each of the six previous shows the old girl had been progressively more unpleasant and the behaviour of the secretaries—always a yardstick by which you could judge your standing in T.T.'s establishment—had become less and less subservient.

Seven shows, thought Christina Scott as she fortified herself for the coming interview with a nip from a bottle tucked away in the boot of her car. Seven shows. Well, my luck's out, that's all. And with T.T. breathing down my neck and making sarcastic remarks I'm losing my self-confidence. I'm too careful; I'm over shortening as I come into my fences; I can feel it, but I can't stop myself and the more I worry the worse it gets. I've lost the knack or something, but if only she'd leave me alone and those cats of secretaries would stop their moronic criticisms. She knew what everyone must be saying behind her back, certainly in the collecting rings and horse-box parks and probably in the enclosures and before the television screens as well: 'Christina's lost her nerve.' 'Christina's on the bottle.' One had heard that sort of thing said so often about people who'd started on the slide down from the top, one had even said it oneself. But that's not what's happened to me; this is only a temporary thing, Christina reassured herself. I've just struck a rough patch; it's impossible to win all the time with the competition as it is today. And then as T.T.'s gaunt and somehow forbidding figure came in sight she slammed the car boot shut and went forward to meet her.

'Sorry, Miss Thistleton, no luck again. We *have* struck a bad patch this time.' She smiled, the wry, sporting smile with which she had been taught to face defeat. The sight of this smile on Christina's square, rather self-satisfied face was too much for Theodora Thistleton; with a sensation of relief she loosed the anger which had been building up in her all day.

'So you think it's bad luck, do you?' she stormed. 'I don't, I know it's your bad riding. I've told you to let them go on more, but of course you know best. Seven shows and not a single prize. And everyone knows what I've paid for those horses. All right, Miss Scott, if you can't win on my horses I'll find someone who can.'

Christina showed no sign of emotion at this attack. Her eyes continued to gaze at T.T. with their usual cool directness, her brown, almost swarthy skin neither flushed nor blenched. 'Of course, I don't think that that little girl groom of yours, Brenda, is giving them nearly enough work,' she said calmly.

'So that's it now, is it? First it was the fences, then it was the hard ground, then the horses were wrongly fed and now you have the impertinence to suggest that they're not exercised. Well, I'm not giving you a chance to try that theory out, I've had enough of being a laughing stock, you've had your last ride on my horses; I'm not going to be humiliated in this way. I shall make other arrangements from today. And, if you take my advice you'll find something else to do for a living, because you're only spoiling good horses and making an exhibition of yourself.' With this T.T. strode away across the showground, her long back still rigid with righteous indignation. Christina looked after her for a moment or two and then opened the boot of the car and helped herself with shaking hands to another nip from the bottle. She doesn't really mean it, she told herself, trying to stem the tide of rising panic. Oh God! I'm finished if she does. No one's offered me a ride for weeks. They used to beg me to jump their animals, she thought bitterly. Now I haven't even the hope of a decent Grade C horse to fall back on. There's the disgrace of it too. T.T.'ll tell everyone that she kicked me out. *Pity and sympathy,* thought Christina with the revulsion of one who has always commanded admiration and respect.

Marion Keswick, huddled on a tip-up seat in the groom's compartment of the horse-box, surrounded by saddlery, grooming tools and buckets and showered with hay seeds each time the horse nearest her pulled at his net, listened with half an ear to T.T.'s dismissal of Christina Scott, but found that, so far from distracting her, Christina's troubles had merely intensified the misery of her own. She could no longer delude herself with the pretence that she was getting over Laurence, that she was making a new life for herself or that things had changed for the better. The sight of him had removed this, the prop of the last two weeks, and left her temporarily defenceless. For as long as T.T.'s horses had needed her ministrations Marion had managed to preserve a facade of normality; she'd saddled, bridled, bandaged and studded-up with grim concentration and, as each horse failed to qualify for its jump-off, she had unsaddled, unbridled, removed studs and prepared them for the journey home, with equal concentration. But now, with only old Grey Miller due in at five, there was nothing left to do and she had hidden herself in the horse-box and given way to her agonized thoughts.

When Theodora Thistleton had telephoned her to ask for her help, explaining that after some 'unpleasantness' her male staff had left in a body and the one girl groom who remained was incapable of driving the horse-box, Marion had cheerfully agreed to help out until new grooms were found, partly because she was in that state of mind when change seems synonymous with progress and partly, though this was unadmitted at the time, because she hoped for a glimpse of Laurence. The glimpse of Laurence had been far from reassuring. Now as she sat in the horse-box, huddled as though cold in spite of the intense heat, the more agonizing moments of the day reproduced themselves. Laurence jumping a clear round, watched admiringly by Helen Farrell. The two heads, dark and fair, close together as Laurence helped Helen with her horse's studs. Laurence standing at the collecting ring entrance and explaining to Helen how she could save several seconds in the Foxhunter jump-off. It would be bad enough with anyone, thought Marion, mopping ineffectively at the slow ooze of tears, but with the notorious Helen, on the loose again since her last divorce . . . Laurence, poor, silly Laurence would be no match for her. Few drifting husbands had withstood the deceptive look of innocence in those wide blue eyes, the rose-bud lips that were always a little parted, revealing two perfect teeth, the long golden hair, which, when it was not bundled under a hunting cap, hung about her face in a carefully arranged confusion.

Pull yourself together, Marion told herself, you can't behave like this. It's all over. You've parted. But she was becoming aware that her body, ignoring common-sense decisions, had a life and determination of its own and, crying out for Laurence's body it managed to suggest that the much vaunted triumph of mind over matter could well be a Pyrrhic victory. Marion sat on, oblivious of everything but the raw ache of her misery until T.T.'s angry face was suddenly framed in the doorway. 'Where's Brenda?' she demanded and then, without waiting for an answer, she added, 'I want the horses taken home at once; Grey Miller won't be jumping in the Fault and Out.'

Laurence Keswick's chief sensation on seeing his wife had been of anger. The irritation of finding her acting as extra dogsbody to his cousin had turned to anger as he realised that the letter he'd received from the interfering old woman that morning had probably been prompted by some confidence of Marion's. No doubt she'd been pouring all her woes and all his iniquities into T.T.'s ear.

His annoyance that their affairs were now known to a third person was increased by the sight of Marion creeping about looking broken and hideous. She always looked hideous when she was unhappy. The small, expressive, slightly monkey-face owed all its attractiveness to her vivacious personality and when her spirit failed there was no bone structure or feature of note to redeem her face from downright ugliness. And God knows when she'd last had her hair done; she was economising again, he thought angrily.

He'd watched her earlier, looking from him to Helen with hurt, reproachful eyes. It was such a dog-in-the-manger attitude. She'd kicked him out—well, more or less—what right had she to complain? At least Helen tried to amuse. She didn't nag or talk perpetually of money. She had a way of making you feel that you were the only man on earth as far as she was concerned, and though you knew you'd be lucky if it lasted six weeks that didn't seem to matter; it was a wonderful antidote to the drear down-to-earthness of married life.

Then realizing that it was almost his turn to jump he tightened his horse's girths, mounted and walked him round. Concentrating all his attention on the ring he made sure he knew the course. They'd altered it for the Fault and Out, made it more complicated with sharper turns, and that treble they'd erected was a real stinker—a gate and a triple followed by parallel bars.

Greedily Mrs. Pratt added up her winnings. The girls had done well today. Between them Sybs and 'Gin had carried off all the junior jumping prizes but the third, and Liz and Top Ten had again won the Foxhunter. It had been a good class—eighty-two entries—but more important than that was the first prize of twenty-five pounds. Now she could pay Old Smiley for the horse-box repairs and stop the constant drain which hiring made on her resources. For the garage, knowing of Mrs. Pratt's pecuniary difficulties, had refused to return her ramshackle, but now roadworthy, horse-box until they were paid for the repairs and Mrs. Pratt was too well known locally to be allowed to hire a cattle truck for anything but ready cash. Now, while the girls tried to pick up a few extra pounds in Ring Two where a children's gymkhana was being held, Mrs. Pratt was staying near the cattle truck to keep an eye on Top Ten. Nothing must happen to him before tomorrow; another win and they'd be clear of the grey pinching poverty of the last few weeks. Not, mused Mrs. Pratt, that the cheques would arrive at once, but if the girls did well in the gymkhana—those were cash prizes—she began to calculate how much she'd be in pocket if the girls won *all* the gymkhana events, which they had done before now, for the well-fed, nicely brought-up Pony Club children were no match for the wiry little Pratts, who knew that their next meal depended upon their efforts.

They'd stop on the way home and buy a joint, thought Mrs. Pratt, and at the thought she felt her salivary glands go into action. Syb's jodhpur boots would have to be mended—the soles were flapping—and perhaps, she thought wistfully, there would be something left for a drink. She climbed up the ramp of the cattle truck and stood looking at her ugly little bay horse with anxious, avaricious eyes. If only they could keep him right; he'd be up-graded before long, of course, but until then he was a real money spinner.

Helen Farrell, free of Farrell the ship's engineer she had fallen for on a cruise round the Greek Islands and married, despite the objections of her father, Lord Creech, had taken up show jumping again as an outlet for her restless energy, while she considered her position and decided on her next move. As a young girl she'd been quite well known and had had two really good horses, but now the price of a Grade A jumper was so exorbitant, she had decided that a promising young horse, which she could ride in Foxhunters and Grade C classes, was all she could possibly afford. Devon Lad had gone well, he'd been seventh today—just in the money. He hadn't touched a fence, it was just that she hadn't liked to hurry him in the jump-off against the clock. If you hurried a youngster too soon he lost his head; you had to wait until they had a bit of experience before you rode all out to win. Now, with her horse boxed and ready for home, she was waiting to see Laurence Keswick jump in the Fault and Out. She looked across the collecting ring at him. Dark and lean and hard; madly attractive, she thought, and possessing all the culture that Jim Farrell had lacked. Poor Jim, she'd allowed sensuality to sweep her away there, but it was quite natural after that long dreary year with Bruce Cordil—her second husband, an immensely rich, but as it turned out, miserly, industrial magnate. The frugal living had soon palled and his baldness, with which she'd been prepared to put up in the expectation of unlimited spending money, had become daily more repulsive. Then there were the endless dinners when she was supposed to make herself pleasant to the most incredible people: poisonous politicians, bulging dithering Lady Mayoresses and the dreary, over-dressed wives of Bruce's business associates; and all she'd got out of it were some very ordinary diamonds. After that it wasn't surprising that she'd begun again convinced that love was all that mattered. But life with Jim hadn't been exactly a bed of roses. Oh, the crashing boredom of having him around all day, those long, long days between the nights of love. Naturally she'd persuaded him to give up his job, of what use was a husband perpetually at sea? She'd assured him that she could pay for everything and how furious he'd been when he found the drawer in the writing-table stuffed with unpaid bills and learned the state of her bank account. Now, though Daddy had forked out a little, the situation was still difficult, especially since she'd bought the horse, Land Rover and trailer and taken up jumping again. She wondered if old T.T. was really going to leave Laurence Keswick her quarter of a million. Laurence had said no, she was just as likely to leave it to a cat's home when it came to the point. And then there was the immediate future. One thing's certain, thought Helen, I'm not marrying just for love again. Whoever wants my body can jolly well pay through the nose for it. Why should women keep on giving, giving, giving, the *whole* time? Men are such selfish brutes.

To Hugh Chesterfield's relief his mother had not been in

her usual high spirits. Instead of excited and voluble she had been quiet and preoccupied and Hugh, who at seventeen believed that one's sole duty in life was to conform to the point of being totally indistinguishable as an individual when among one's own sort, had been spared hours of gnawing embarrassment. Normally, his younger sister's epic jump-off against the Pratts would have sent his mother scurrying round amongst her friends and acquaintances to recount each moment in a loud, excitable voice. She expected equal enthusiasm from her listeners and was quite unaware that however pleased they felt about Sarah's successes, few of them could raise any interest in her accounts of how each contestant jumped every fence, whether they took off too soon or too late or whether it was just bad luck that they'd had a brick off the wall. But today she'd hardly spoken to her friends and even her denunciations of the Pratts' pot-hunting habits had lacked their usual force and gusto.

Hugh, bored stiff, for he had given up riding two years ago, sweltering in the suit he had worn from the sheer terror of being incorrectly dressed in anything else, had sat all day in the enclosure, while his mother, short, square, grey-haired and wearing, he thanked God, a cotton dress and not those unspeakable jeans, had bustled backwards and forwards, plying her children with food and drink, helping Sarah with studs, holding the pony while she visited the Ladies, offering advice and support. Now he saw her at the enclosure entrance signalling to him grotesquely. He got up and threading his way through the mostly untenanted deck chairs, he wondered bitterly why she couldn't behave like other people. 'Come on,' she called loudly. 'We're all boxed up and ready to go. And for goodness' sake take that coat off, Hughie, you look like a boiled lobster.'

'I'm not in the least hot,' he answered stiffly.

The Upshott Show was a first venture, the result of the Council's determination to put Upshott, a new town built mainly to house part of London's overspill, on the map.

In a sudden access of civic pride they had decided that whatever Windsor could do, they could do better and they'd embarked on preparations for a two-day show. Certainly the arrangements were excellent. The enclosures, the parking facilities, the fences and the prize money had all been provided on a lavish scale. The competitors had entered in numbers that threatened to disorganize the programme, but spectators, there were almost none. The town councillors, sitting in their reserved seats and mopping their brows as they watched their wives, resplendent in especially purchased summer outfits, handing out cups and rosettes, blamed the poor attendance on the intense heat and hoped that Saturday would bring more temperate weather and a large crowd, to save them from charges of having squandered the ratepayers' money. But Saturday was equally hot. Some people, ignoring scientific evidence, insisted that it was hotter. The refreshment tent ran out of beer and soft drinks; the ice-cream vans ran a shuttle service between their depot and the showground. Tempers were frayed; the competitors questioned the judges' decisions; the show-jumping judges quarrelled over the course for the Grade C class, old General Gateley went home in a dudgeon and left the other two to struggle through the rest of the programme without a relief. The chief ring steward sulked and the course builder retired to the refreshment tent and, over a succession of gin and tonics, composed furious letters to the British Show Jumping Association.

Theodora Thistleton had engaged young Billy Brown to ride her horses. At nineteen he'd just appeared among the top show-jumping riders, having had a tremendously successful season, including several spectacular wins at the International Show. But the sudden transition from Christina Scott's over-careful placing to Brown's fast, rather wild style was too much for the Thistleton horses. They galloped round in a confused manner, taking off haphazardly and as the fences fell T.T.'s expression grew grim; it was to be her eighth show without a rosette.

But if Theodora Thistleton was angry and disappointed, Betty Pratt was in a state bordering on despair, for Top Ten, saddled and ready for the Grade C jumping, had had to be withdrawn at the last minute, apparently lame. Mrs. Pratt was certain that the lameness was in the off fore, but the little knot of grooms, competitors and veterinary know-alls that always gathers when a horse is run out, disagreed. Almost to a man they insisted that it was the near fore the horse was saving. Liz Pratt said it couldn't be much, perhaps he'd just trodden on a stone, but Mrs. Pratt, showing a solicitude that seemed out of character, announced that she wasn't going to risk a horse's soundness by jumping him when he wasn't one hundred per cent and put him back in the box. For the rest of the day she was in one of her blackest moods. Sybil had her face slapped for taking the wrong course in the Junior Hit and Hurry and wasting a ten shilling entrance fee and the fact that Virginia was only second added to Mrs. Pratt's anger. Liz, who'd decided that if Top Ten won again, a long-desired stiffened petticoat and perhaps a pair of shoes with stiletto heels were to be her share of the spoils, sulked, squabbled endlessly with Sybil and finally fought with Virginia, who had taken an unfairly large bite out of the ice-cream cornet they were sharing. Rolling on the grass kicking, biting, scratching and hair lolling, they fought like tigers and screamed like cats, at last to be forcibly separated by a pair of disapproving cattle-truck drivers who thought that the undignified scene had gone on long enough.

Laurence Keswick had better luck, he won the Upshott Shield and the fifty pounds presented by the Chamber of Commerce which went with it and on the strength of this he offered to take Helen Farrell out to dinner. Marion, observing Laurence's unmistakable air of happiness and Helen's increasingly affectionate manner towards him, was appalled by the strength of her own feelings; it was incredible that she, who had always considered herself a mild, kindly person, was suffering this bitter jealousy, this frightening, soul-consuming sensation of hate.

The behaviour of the Browns added to Marion's misery. In their anxiety to put up some sort of show with T.T.'s horses they hotted the unfortunate animals up into a state of frenzy; martingales were shortened and nose-bands tightened before young Billy mounted and warmed them up with liberal, though surreptitious, use of spurs and a cutting whip. Then, just before each horse was due to enter the ring, he was put over the practice jump which had been moved behind the box out of sight of stewards and passers-by—and 'rapped' by father Brown and a confederate who, holding a heavy pole between them, crashed it against the horse's legs in an attempt to make him jump higher and with more care.

The secretaries passed a very exhausting day. In the morning, it was true that T.T. had allowed them to sit in the enclosure for quite a long time while she wandered about the showground alone, but after lunch she became extremely fractious; sending them perpetually in pursuit of cooling drinks which were obtained with great difficulty and which always failed to please; demanding insect repellent, anti-sunburn lotion and then an umbrella, so that they never ceased scurrying backwards and forwards, except when they were moving her deck chair into what *might* be a cooler spot. By five o'clock they both felt themselves to be bordering on a state of nervous collapse and, when T.T. demanded the thermos of milk shake that was in the horse-box, for a few moments neither secretary moved.

'My thermos, *please*.' T.T. sensed mutiny and her eyes blazed with anger as she repeated her request. Once again it was Molly Steer who, dreading unpleasantness, especially in public, gave way first.

'Yes, Miss Thistleton,' she answered wearily and set off across the hot dusty showground. She was away a long time. T.T. fidgeted impatiently, grumbled unceasingly and finally sent a reluctant Joy Hemming to investigate. The secretaries returned together. Molly, hot and flustered, explained almost incoherently that she had been unable to find the basket at first for someone had moved it.

'You can never see an inch in front of your nose,' snapped T.T. disagreeably. 'Now come on, don't stand there, pour me out a drink.' She sighed impatiently as Molly fumbled with the stopper, snatched the cup when at last the pink liquid was poured and drank deeply. A look of surprise crossed her face. 'I feel—' she began but before she could finish her sentence her face turned white; her breathing changed to long strangled gasps and, as the secretaries stared at her with alarmed faces, she pitched forward, dropping the cup, and slipped in a sagging heap from the deck chair to the ground.

'She's fainted,' said Molly Steer.

'Loosen her scarf; put her head between her knees,' directed Joy Hemming. But the scarf was already loose and the long unwieldy body only sprawled grotesquely when Molly tried to prop it up. The chalk-white face, the staring eyes, the long shuddering breaths, frightened them both.

'You'd better run for a doctor,' said Joy and obediently Molly Steer set off, shambling and panting towards the Show Secretary's tent. Pushing her way through an angry group of competitors who were objecting to the winner of the Grade C class, she managed to stammer out that a doctor was needed urgently in the enclosure. The Secretary picked up his field telephone and as she emerged from the tent, having pushed her way back through the objectors, she heard the announcer calling Dr. Fitzgerald. When she got back to the enclosure she found T.T. already covered with a rug and lying in a space cleared of deck chairs, with the doctor, a short, fat man who'd been located in the bar, kneeling beside her. Two St. John Ambulance men cleared more chairs to make room for a stretcher.

As they hurried her to the ambulance, Dr. Fitzgerald tried to learn the background of the collapse from Joy, and Molly, suddenly becoming aware of her employer's likely reactions should she return to consciousness and find herself in the general ward of Upshott Hospital, began to plead for nursing homes and private rooms. But the doctor, watching them load T.T. and looking from her body, struggling to draw each laborious breath, to the froth that had appeared on her lips, snapped, '*If* she does return to consciousness she'll be a very lucky woman. I'm going to telephone the hospital; you'd better go with her.'

At the hospital they injected and stomach-pumped in vain. Twenty minutes later, just as Laurence Keswick rode in to jump in the final class, Theodora Thistleton died.

CHAPTER TWO

THE STAFF of Upshott's gleaming and still unfinished hospital were in no doubt that Theodora Thistleton had died from poisoning and no sooner was the battle for her life lost, than they telephoned the Coroner and the pathologist. Half an hour later a police sergeant appeared to collect the thermos and he also took statements from both secretaries, who were then allowed to return to Whittam. By the time they sat down to eat their over-cooked supper—it was macaroni cheese, a favourite dish of T.T.'s—the pathologist, summoned from spraying his roses, was already at work.

On Sunday the heat was even more oppressive and people, looking at the darkening blue of the sky, spoke hopefully of a storm. The secretaries, having contacted Theodora Thistleton's solicitor and arranged for announcements of her death in *The Times* and the *Telegraph*, had no occupation but answering the telephone and that was unsatisfactory, since they could tell inquirers only that T.T. was dead and the police investigating. Between the calls they bickered. Molly, in her desire to wear something dark, was sweltering in a grey skirt and brown jersey; she had even found a few tears to shed and went about the house on tiptoe, drawing curtains, 'out of respect,' she said, 'for the dead.'

Joy, maintaining that this behaviour was hypocritical, clattered round after her undrawing the curtains and protesting loudly. Mrs. Maggs served two meals of cold mutton and pink blancmange and Brenda Dix turned all the show jumpers out in a field to exercise themselves and decided to leave the mucking out until Monday.

At half-past two on Monday afternoon Detective-Superintendent Jackson, head of the County Police Criminal Investigation Department, received the toxicologist's report and learned that Theodora Thistleton had died from hydrocyanic acid administered in the pink milk shake. At three he discussed the case with his new Chief Constable, Colonel Murray. Jackson, a large moody man with a domed forehead, scanty grey hair, dark pouches under small eyes and an enormous bony nose, had worked his way up from a constable and felt aggrieved that Murray should have reached his present position by way of the Kenya Police. In Jackson's opinion it made mockery of the theory that the police force was now a closed service. But he was due to retire in three months' time so he had pushed his antagonism under the surface and contented himself by running his department with as little reference to the Chief as possible and by an occasional spiteful remark if Murray showed ignorance on some point of police procedure.

Murray, for his part, thought Jackson out of date and intended a reorganization of the C.I.D. as soon as he retired; meanwhile he left Jackson perpetually short-handed by sending his staff on training courses.

Murray was taller than Jackson, but of much lighter build. He had brown hair, from which nothing would remove a tight corkscrew curl, parted on one side and brushed straight across his flat-topped head. His face was wide at the brow but narrowed abruptly, his eyes were alert-looking and blue, but the expression on his face was generally one of worried stupidity.

'With both Smith and Henty on courses I suppose I shall have to deal with this myself,' Jackson began aggressively. 'Of course there's Craker, but as it is he's working overtime on this fire raiser and getting nowhere fast.'

'Yes, I think you ought to deal with it, I mean murder's a serious business. You could let that new chap Roper help you, he seems keen and it would give him some valuable experience.'

'Well now, what have we got so far?'

Both men opened their folders. 'Ah, hydrocyanic acid, that sounds like wasps' nests. Been a bad summer for wasps so there's probably plenty of it about; we'd better send a man round the chemists.' Murray glowed with self-satisfaction at having produced this contribution.

'Yes, but which chemists?' asked Jackson. 'There's no reason to suppose that the poison came from Upshott or Hamberley, or Whittam where Miss Thistleton lived. The riders at that horse show came from all over the place, in fact in the George last night they were telling me there was certainly one from Wales, several from Somerset and they thought that Gloucestershire, Warwickshire and Northampton were represented too.'

'Um, that does complicate things a bit,' Murray admitted. 'Well, I suppose we'll have to narrow down the suspects a bit before we start to follow up the "access to poison" angle.'

'I'm going over to Whittam now to interview the household,' Jackson told him. 'I'll begin by finding out who could have tampered with that drink. We've one or two prints from the thermos, so I'll take Caley with me to fingerprint all those who admit to handling it. Do you want me to take young Roper too?' he asked as he heaved himself to his feet.

'Yes.' Murray wished that Jackson wouldn't make it sound as though he were doing a favour every time he obeyed an order, but he reminded himself—only three months more. 'Oh, and report to me when you get back,' he added, 'and if I've left phone me at home.'

Jackson grunted as he left the room. He sent for Sergeant Caley and a police car and collected Roper, a fair, gangling, pink and white youth, from the office where, because he was one of the Chief's bright boys, he had kept him, since his appointment from the uniformed branch, on the dreariest of administrative duties.

They drove westward from Hamberley, through pine and rhododendron country, along a main road edged with one of those opulent ribbon developments of the twenties, each substantial house almost secluded in pine-sheltered garden. Whittam, once a small village, had been engulfed by this rich crawling suburbia, but Whittam House itself was late Victorian. A red-brick unsymmetrical horror with strange turrets and other unnecessary excrescences, it looked away from the road over a sloping lawn, but the drive and the other three sides of the house were shrouded in a mass of conifer and evergreens which would normally have seemed dark and gloomy, but in the heat offered a deep, delightful shade. Jackson rang the bell and waited.

Then, just as he was about to ring again, the door opened and three women began to explain at once why he had been kept waiting.

'Detective-Superintendent Jackson of the County Police,' Jackson ignored the explanations and announced himself loudly. 'I imagine you ladies must be the secretaries?' he added, walking into the dark-panelled hall and depositing his hat on a chair.

'That's right. I'm Miss Hemming.'

'I'm Miss Steer.' both secretaries tried to identify themselves at once.

'And this lady?' asked Jackson, looking at a thin, bespectacled woman in her late fifties with the withdrawn face of the deaf and wild grey hair.

"That's Mrs. Maggs, Miss Thistleton's cook,' Joy Hemming told him.

'Are there any other staff?' asked Jackson.

'No, only Miss Dix, that's what I was trying to explain to you only Miss Steer would interrupt—'

'I didn't interrupt, Joy, how can you be so unkind? It was just that I was trying to tell him too.' Molly Steer's face flushed with indignation.

'You did interrupt,' Joy contradicted. 'I didn't,' Molly began, but Jackson said, 'Yes, yes, yes,' in loud and testy tones, and having silenced them, added, 'I'd like to run through the statements you made to the Upshott police with you ladies presently, but first I want to talk to Mrs. Maggs. Meanwhile Sergeant Caley can take your finger-prints—if you've no objection—we want to find out whether any outsiders handled the thermos. Now where can I talk to Mrs. Maggs?'

'In the morning-room'—'In the drawing-room'—Both secretaries spoke at once.

'Well, which is it to be?' asked Jackson impatiently.

Joy seized the initiative. 'Mrs. Maggs, the Superintendent wants to see you in the morning-room,' she shouted.

'All right, Miss 'Emming, I 'eard. I'm not that deaf,' Mrs. Maggs answered sharply. 'This way, please,' she said to Jackson.

Jackson turned to his staff. 'That'll be four sets of prints then, Caley. Come on, Roper, I want you.'

Mrs. Maggs led them into a large and somehow cheerless room which looked eastward across a strip of lawn to the surrounding conifers. It was crowded with solid, useful pieces of heavily carved oak furniture and metal filing cabinets flanking a kneehole desk revealed that it was used as an office. The floor was polished and rug-scattered, the ornaments all of horses. The row of silver cups on the chimney-piece had been won by horses and the walls were hung with pictures of horses. Half a dozen were indifferent oil paintings and the rest mainly photographs, many of them coloured.

'You sit at the table, Roper,' directed Jackson, and turning to Mrs. Maggs he asked, 'Full name?'

When Mrs. Maggs answered, 'Yes, time we did, no vegetables and everything so dusty,' he pulled his nose angrily and decided that it was going to be a difficult interview. Eventually he learned that on Saturday she had prepared the milk shake in exactly the same way as usual. The milk was from the usual milkman, the flavouring from the usual bottle, and the spoonful of ice cream had been taken from a newly opened carton. She had beaten the mixture in the electric mixer and poured it into a thermos which had stood in the refrigerator, until it was time to put it on the table in the hall for the secretaries to pack the basket which they always took to horse shows. Mrs. Maggs had been with Miss Thistleton for a year and neither liked nor disliked her employer, but she didn't, she said, 'care for the secretaries'. She had no idea why anyone should want to murder Miss Thistleton, she had seen no strangers hanging round the house and she was quite certain in her own mind that if Miss Thistleton had been poisoned, it was through eating something from the refreshment tent at the show.

Jackson asked her to send Miss Steer next and almost at once they heard Molly scurrying down the passage in an anxious endeavour not to keep the Superintendent waiting. She burst into the room flustered and breathless, stumbled over a rug and only just saved herself from falling by grabbing an occasional table; the objects on the table slid to the floor with a crash. 'Oh dear, how *clumsy* of me,' cried Molly, crimson-faced and in abject distress. 'Oh dear, it's broken, Miss Thistleton's *favourite* china horse. Oh, I *am* sorry.' Painstakingly she began to collect the bits. 'Perhaps it could be glued.' Jackson pulled his nose impatiently.

'Never mind about that now, Miss Steer. Come and sit down.' Clutching the shattered horse tenderly Molly sat where she was told, but she was so busy reproaching herself for her clumsiness and lack of poise that she was quite unable to concentrate on either Jackson's questions or her own answers. She debated endlessly and ineffectively whether T.T. had really had her last lemonade going to the Ladies tent or afterwards and each time she was prevailed upon to commit herself to a definite statement of fact, she immediately began to wonder whether the incident hadn't taken place on Friday and not Saturday after all. The only points Jackson managed to pin her down on concerned her own actions. She had taken the thermos from the hall table, packed it in what was known as the emergency basket, seen it into the hired car and then, on arrival at the show, into the groom's compartment of the horse-box. She had visited the horsebox at least once that afternoon, for she was quite certain that it was on Saturday that she had fetched the insect repellent and not Friday—she distinctly remembered Miss Thistleton being bitten by a horsefly. She had also fetched the thermos and poured out the milk shake.

After Mrs. Maggs and Molly Steer, Joy Hemming was a model witness. She was both calm and helpful, but Jackson viewed her with repugnance. She was so small and faded; so dowdy in low-heeled shoes and an unfashionably long dress. Not that Jackson liked any women; the shameful memories of a brief marriage when he had found himself to be impotent, though now buried deep, still coloured his outlook and, except for very elegant, well-dressed and made-up women whose company could sometimes send a tiny surge of virility through him, he found them all repellent.

With much scuffling among the filing system, Joy Hemming produced the names and addresses of the three women who came each morning to help with the house-work and the names and, as far as she knew them, addresses of all the staff who had left so abruptly. It was, she explained, over T.T.'s treatment of Williams, the old butler, who had put up with her for so much longer than anyone else, that the trouble had come about.

'It seems that Miss Thistleton was very rude to him; he wouldn't tell anyone exactly what she said, but she was often very sarcastic and if she was in one of her really nasty moods she would even go so far as to use bad language,' Joy explained to Jackson. 'Anyway, according to Williams's story, he told her quite politely that she oughtn't to speak to him like that because he was a servant and not supposed to answer back. T.T. promptly sacked him—he'd been here donkey's years—and insisted that he left the same night. The rest of the staff—the stud groom and his son the chauffeur, the housemaids, all gave notice at once. Only Mrs. Maggs, who's really a bit dotty, poor dear, and Brenda Dix, the little girl groom, who has a local boy friend, decided to stay and at the end of the week the others all went. I think T.T. expected them to give way right up to the last, for she wouldn't let us advertise for new staff.'

'And this Mrs. Keswick who was driving the horse-box?' asked Jackson.

'T.T. asked her to help out, she's really a sort of relation. At least she's married to Laurence Keswick, who was a cousin of some sort.'

'Ah, now that's interesting. I understand from the solicitors that a Mr. Laurence Keswick is the chief beneficiary under Miss Thistleton's will. Drew, Nittard and Drew, I think it was you who told them to telephone the police?'

'Yes, we telephoned Mr. Drew to tell him the terrible

news on Sunday and he seemed to think it impossible that any client of his could have died in, well, peculiar circumstances; he seemed to think we were a couple of hysterical women,' Joy smiled whimsically, 'so we suggested that he should ring the County Police.'

'Husband and wife, eh?' said Jackson pulling his nose gently.

'Yes, but I don't know for how much longer; they've parted and I believe they're thinking of divorce. Such a pity.'

Jackson had asked for Marion Keswick's address and then returned to the thermos. Joy Hemming agreed that Molly Steer had put it into the basket, taken the basket to the car, transferred it to the horse-box. 'Why was it kept in the horse-box?' asked Jackson. 'As far as I can make out you ladies spent the day going backwards and forwards fetching things. Why didn't you have it all in the enclosure with you?'

Joy laughed. 'You don't realise what T.T. was like,' she said. 'She always insisted on travelling about with everything she might possibly need. Some of the things we had to drag round with us we've never used since I've been here and that's two years. Mackintoshes and rugs even in a spell of hot weather like we're having now, air cushions, shooting stick, umbrella and of course the "emergency" basket, stuffed with first-aid kits, safety pins, aspirins and all the rest of it. Normally we'd leave it all in the car and fetch it as required, you couldn't carry it all around with you, but with no chauffeur she had to hire a car and Mr. Brain, he's the local man, didn't want to sit about at the show all day and for that matter I don't think T.T. particularly wanted to pay him for doing nothing. It wasn't as though the show was far away, you see, Upshott to Whittam, what is it? About nine miles?'

'So the thermos was in the horse-box in the care of Mrs. Keswick and Miss Dix until at approximately five o'clock Miss Steer went to fetch it?'

'Yes,' Joy smiled whimsically. 'I think she was just a wee bit put out. You see she's very particular about dividing all our duties up and doing them turn and turn about; I think life's too short for that sort of thing really, sometimes one does more, and sometimes the other, but I do try to remember the turns as it means so much to Molly; when T.T. wanted the thermos I think Molly thought it was my turn, she looked very put out, but really and truly I'd been to the horse-box not long before to fetch the anti-sunburn lotion when T.T. thought the sun was catching her face.'

'Mr. Drew tells me that Miss Thistleton asked him to come down and see her next Thursday,' said Jackson. 'Any idea what it was about?'

'Well, I do know a little about it and I suppose it wouldn't be betraying a confidence now. Though of course it might not have come to anything because she often threatened to do something in a rage and then did something quite different when she'd cooled down.'

'Yes, yes,' Jackson pulled his nose; this female was more coherent than the other one, but he'd never known anyone so long-winded, he'd begun to pity Miss Thistleton spending her life cooped up with the pair of them and paying and feeding them too.

'You see,' Joy's voice had become confidential, 'T.T.

was very disgusted with Laurence Keswick. It seemed she disapproved of divorce, anyway she wrote to him. She wrote herself, it wasn't a typewritten letter so we didn't see it, except just for the envelope. I took it to the post. Then we had to write and ask Mr. Drew to come down and she began to drop hints that she was thinking of leaving her money to the Chesterfield children, well, they're not exactly children now, Hugh's seventeen and I think Sarah's fifteen.'

'Are they any relation?' asked Jackson.

'No, none at all. Laurence Keswick's her only relation, I believe.'

'Hum.' Jackson heaved himself to his feet. 'Before I see Miss Dix, I'd like to take a look round the kitchen.'

Jackson's appearance in the kitchen and the fact that he took possession of the bottle which contained the milk shake flavouring—the milk had long since been drunk and the ice cream eaten—threw Mrs. Maggs into a violent unreasoning fear. She began to mutter incoherent protestations of innocence and Jackson, finding that however loudly he bawled, 'It's just a routine check-up. The laboratory will just make sure there was nothing wrong with the flavouring,' he could not reach her, shrugged his shoulders and asked where he would find Miss Dix. 'Miss Steer'll show you the way,' Joy told him. 'Molly, you'll take the Superintendent to the stables, won't you, dear?' she added, cornering the obviously reluctant Molly in the hall.

As she led Jackson and Roper down the gravel path through the conifers Molly Steer was at first speechless with embarrassment, but by the time they reached the stable-yard she had begun to apologize at great length for the clumsiness of her entrance to the morning-room. She seemed much afflicted by what the Superintendent must think of her. Jackson couldn't find it in him to offer any comfort so he only answered, 'Yes, yes, yes,' in testy tones and pulled his nose.

They found Brenda Dix and Sergeant Caley giggling up in the little flat. Fingerprinting had proved an excellent introduction and the brown-eyed, Latin-looking Caley was a fast worker. Brenda, a dazzlingly artificial blonde, was wearing a pink sleeveless blouse, apple green jeans and a pair of rather dusty patent-leather chisel-toed flattie shoes. Jackson took one look and began to pull his nose violently; he detested women in shorts, slacks, coloured stockings, huge hairy sweaters or in any other form of mildly unconventional dress.

'Miss Dix?' he asked, and as Brenda gave him a charming smile he turned hastily away. 'Come on, Roper, come on. Aren't you ready yet?' he demanded as young Roper searched for his pen.

'Full names,' he barked at Brenda.

'Brenda Joyce Dix,' she answered, flashing a smile at Roper.

'On Saturday you went to the Upshott Show in a horsebox driven by Mrs. Keswick?'

'Yes, that's right,' agreed Brenda.

'Shortly after your arrival Miss Steer brought various objects including a basket and put them in the groom's compartment of the horse-box?'

'That's right, we'd been there some time, mind you. Mrs. Keswick thought we ought to get there in plenty of time because Billy Brown had never ridden any of the horses before and she thought he'd want plenty of time to have a ride round and get used to them. But not him. Full of himself, he was; said Christina Scott didn't know how to ride them and he'd soon get them going again. Ever so rough he was. Cruel I call it. I was surprised really at old T.T. letting a boy like that ride them, she's generally so particular, but I suppose she wanted to win. And then they crack him up enough; he's always got his picture in the papers; you'd think he was Adam Faith or Pat Smythe or someone really famous, but he's not a bit like that, I think he's stupid really; he got nothing to say for himself.'

'Now this basket,' said Jackson, as soon as she drew breath. 'Did you touch it at all or see anyone else touch it?'

'No, we called it every name under the sun, though, well, not just the basket but it and all the other stuff Miss Steer dumped in. You see there were all the horses' rugs and tack and brushes and buckets as well—we couldn't move. And old T.T. she was very particular, always liked to see it all kept up together; you'd soon have her after you if she thought anything might get lost or pinched. Funny really, I mean she had plenty of money.'

'Now you're quite sure you didn't touch the basket?' Jackson didn't believe that this chattering girl had realised the importance of his question.

'No, I had plenty to do rubbing down the horses when Billy Brown had finished with them—dripping they were and of course we'd forgotten the sweat scraper.'

'Did you see Mrs. Keswick touch the basket?' Jackson

was pulling his nose angrily and his voice was growing louder.

'No, well I tell you I didn't pay any attention to the basket, I was kept that busy. Christina Scott, she never does a hand's turn and however rushed you are she never helps out, but she doesn't make work, if you see what I mean, she wouldn't bring the horses back in that state.'

'Did you see anyone hanging round who had no business to be there; any strangers?' asked Jackson.

'No, a few kids came round wanting Billy Brown's autograph, silly really—I mean who's he?'

'Well, that's all, Miss Dix,' said Jackson thankfully, and he led the way down the steep wooden stairs, cursing a case that produced such a number of talkative women. They stopped at Whittam's pseudo-Elizabethan teashop for a quick cup of tea and then drove on to Cranley Common. Cranley was also an overgrown village, but the growth was not as affluent as at Whittam. Here it was bungalows, each with its concrete path, its carefully tended patch of lawn, which surrounded the common. It was obvious from the painted woodwork, the gay curtains and the neat gates that each building was dear to its owners as a haven and home, but the combined result was an eyesore, a long, straggling, unaesthetic mess of red brick, concrete and link wire. Beyond the Common the road wound upwards through a wood and emerged on a bare hillside. Cranley Down had none of the magnificence of real downland, the area was too small, too intersected with wire fences and scattered with smallholdings. The view was of the main road, its rash of petrol stations and ramshackle cafés and, in the distance, the orderly but uninspiring panorama of Upshott New Town.

Down End Farm proved to be one of the smallholdings and Jackson was surprised that the heir to T.T.'s supposed quarter of a million should live in such shoddy surroundings. 'Well, he's certainly getting a bit of a leg up then,' he observed as the police car bumped down the short, rutted lane and stopped at the red-brick box of a house. In the yard an effort had evidently been made with unpromising material for the breeze-block buildings had been whitewashed and a pink geranium flowered in a pot fixed to the wall. The garden was cultivated, but the hard-baked soil had only yielded a very meagre crop and the lawn, like the unshaded fields round the house, was brown and parched and bare. A white bull terrier rose from the doorstep where she was sunning herself and came towards the three detectives. Sergeant Caley, who was in the rear, hung back by the gate and called, 'Look out, those dogs are real terrors for biting,' but Jackson, who never lacked physical courage, walked on firmly, saying over his shoulder, 'They only bite people who are afraid of them and I'm not.' The dog sniffed his legs and then began to wag her tail enthusiastically. 'She can smell my cats,' said Jackson, knocking on the open front door.

Marion Keswick had looked defeated and untidy on Saturday at the show, but now, surprised by her unexpected visitors, she looked even worse. Her fair hair, which had been cut for an over-ambitious style by the Whittam hairdresser, hung lank and uneven, her face, which had not been made up since morning, was devoid of powder and lipstick. She was pale and drawn with sleepless or dream-ridden nights and her blue eyes, that were almost violet-coloured, held a look of deep pain. To Jackson's disgust she wore a pair of crumpled linen slacks with an unmended tear at the knee and a shirt of faded blue.

'Mrs. Keswick?' he asked. And when Marion answered, 'Yes,' in a listless voice, he added, 'Detective-Superintendent Jackson of the County Police. I wish to interview you in connection with the death of Miss Thistleton.'

'Oh yes,' said Marion in the same listless voice. 'Will you come in?' The detectives disposed themselves about the small, square sitting-room. It was pleasantly furnished in white and green and the three good pieces of furniture which the Keswicks possessed, but the effect was marred by the sallow yellow of a tiled fireplace and the fact that Marion had not done any housework for several days; the tables were covered with a thick layer of dust, the green hearthrug with the dog's white hairs.

'Full names,' said Jackson, as soon as he had lowered himself into an armchair.

'Marion Lorraine Keswick,' she answered.

'And on Saturday you drove Miss Thistleton's horse-box to Upshott Show?'

'Yes,' Marion agreed.

'Were you employed to do this?' Jackson asked.

'No. I was just asked to help in an emergency and I said that I would.'

'You knew Miss Thistleton well then?'

'As you probably know, my husband is related to her,'

answered Marion.

'Yes, I understand he is the chief beneficiary under her will,' said Jackson rather sharply. 'Did you know this?'

'Well, yes,' Marion admitted, 'she had told my husband, but he always felt she might easily quarrel with him or change her mind; he didn't count on it.'

'Hmn.' Jackson managed to look and sound unbelieving. 'Do you remember Miss Steer putting various objects including a basket into the groom's compartment of the horse-box?' he asked.

'Yes.'

'Did you handle or open the basket?'

'No.'

'Did you see anyone else handling it?'

'The secretaries appeared and scuffled in it from time to time.'

'No one else?'

'I didn't see anyone else.'

'Did you see anyone enter the box or standing about near it who had no business to be there?'

Marion put her hand to her forehead and thought. 'No, I don't think so,' she answered.

'Was the box left unattended at all?'

'Oh yes, we had four horses there and Billy Brown had some of his father's to jump too, so while he was riding one of them Brenda and I would both be waiting in the collecting ring each holding one of ours. We stayed to watch them jump and then took them away afterwards.'

Jackson pulled his nose and turned to look out of the window. 'I understand that you and your husband are living apart,' he said. 'Is this to be a permanent arrangement?'

'I don't know,' Marion answered, trying to control the quivering of her face.

Jackson tugged fiercely at his nose. He particularly disliked women in tears and he felt that this one was very near them. His voice became sharper. 'How long is it since you parted?' he demanded.

'About a fortnight,' answered Marion.

'And have you communicated with each other since then?'

'He sent me his address, so that I could forward any letters.'

'He didn't tell you about a letter he had from Miss Thistleton?'

'No.'

'You're sure that you haven't written or spoken to each other since you parted?'

'Quite sure,' answered Marion.

'Well now, Mrs. Keswick, if you would just let Sergeant Caley take your fingerprints, it's a help if we have the prints of everyone who was entitled to be in the horse-box.'

When Caley had done Jackson said, 'Just one more thing, can you give me your husband's address?'

'Yes.' Marion went to the writing desk and brought out a postcard. 'You can have this, I can remember it,' she said. 'I don't think he's actually living there, but the horses are there and he's using it as a base.'

'The Brookley Riding Stables, Brookley Green, Hamberley,' read Jackson. 'He hasn't gone far then?'

'No. Well, you see the horses are entered for the

shows round here so those are the ones he has to jump at. Very few shows will take late entries nowadays and anyway the entry fees are too expensive to waste.'

'Does this mean that Mr. Keswick was at the Upshott Show too?' asked Jackson sharply.

'Yes, he was there.'

'Both days?'

'Yes.'

'And you never spoke to each other?' Jackson sounded frankly incredulous.

'Not a word,' answered Marion, struggling for self-control.

'I find that hard to believe.'

'It's true,' Marion told him, but her shaky voice did not carry much conviction.

'Well, thank you, Mrs. Keswick.' Jackson heaved himself out of the chair. 'I expect we shall be round to see you again in a day or two. You're not thinking of going away?'

'No,' said Marion, 'I can't. Somebody's got to feed the pigs and chickens.'

'Stop at the first telephone kiosk,' Jackson told Caley as soon as they were in the car. 'There was one on that common,' and he began to hunt in his pockets. At the kiosk he handed Roper four pennies and the postcard with Keswick's address. 'Find out the number,' he said, 'ring 'em up and ask for Keswick. Tell him that Superintendent Jackson would like to see him at Hamberley Police Station at once. We may get him that way before he has a chance to talk to her.'

Roper spent a long time in the kiosk and finally

returned to report a failure. 'He's not there. They say he's fed his horses and gone and they don't expect to see him until 8 a.m. tomorrow.' Jackson swore. 'Did they know where he'd gone?' 'No, I asked but the chap laughed and said Keswick had taken a pretty girl out to dinner and if he did know where he wouldn't tell me as they wouldn't want to be disturbed.'

Back at Hamberley Jackson found to his delight that the Chief Constable had already left so he was able to look through the contents of his 'In' tray and read the latest report on the arson case in peace, while Caley worked on the fingerprints. Then he went home. He fed his two enormous neutered tabby cats and ate his supper, put ready by the woman who came in daily to do the housework, before he brought himself to telephone the Chief Constable.

'The most interesting thing we've got are the fingerprints on the thermos,' he told Murray. 'They belong to the cook and one of the secretaries, she poured out the drink, and to the woman who drove the horse-box.' 'What's so interesting about that?' asked Murray. 'Aren't they precisely the prints you'd expect to find?' 'Yes,' answered Jackson, 'except for the driver's. We've only got one of hers and it's not a very good one but Caley's found his sixteen points of resemblance.'

'Well, and what's so significant about that?' asked Murray coldly.

'Only that she said she never handled the basket, much less the thermos, and her husband inherits the best part of a quarter of a million,' answered Jackson in triumph.

CHAPTER THREE

IN THE SMALL HOURS of Tuesday morning the long spell of hot weather broke with a violent thunderstorm that crashed and rumbled round the Hamberley, Upshott and Whittam area until daybreak. The torrential rain, unable to soak into the hard-baked ground, lay everywhere in pools, trees were struck by lightning and in several villages the electricity supply failed, but in the morning the fresh, cool air, the smell of wet earth and the rejoicing plants and trees made all but the most avid sun-worshippers welcome the change.

Jackson, having despatched Sergeant Caley to interview Miss Thistleton's daily women and arranged for the appropriate police forces to trace the departed staff and check their whereabouts on Saturday, collected Roper and a car and set off for Brookley Green.

They found the stables down a side road just outside the village; a large, newly painted sign indicated a square of shabby wooden loose-boxes, but, when they left the car they found that the establishment was evidently more prosperous than it looked, for the stable yard was full of children—mostly girls—and ponies. They were about to depart on a ride and a general tightening of girths was punctuated by the cries of those whose ponies had retaliated with nips. Jackson, looking round for an adult, located a youthful riding instructress and making his way through the ponies asked, 'Is Mr. Keswick here this morning?'

'Mr. Keswick? Yes, he's just doing his horses. Look, in that loose-box over there.' Dodging through the rest of the children, who were now mostly mounted and calling out for help in adjusting their stirrups to the right length, Jackson reached the loose-box.

Inside was a large bay horse, which with villainous expression and much exposure of huge yellow teeth snapped at the air and the door and almost at Jackson as it submitted to having its stomach groomed.

'Mr. Keswick?' asked Jackson. The man in the loosebox stopped grooming and straightened up and at once the horse assumed a mild, almost benign expression.

'Yes, that's right.' Keswick came to the door.

'Detective-Superintendent Jackson, County Police. I would like to interview you in connection with the death of Miss Thistleton,' said Jackson. 'Is there anywhere here where we can talk undisturbed?'

Keswick scratched his head and looked round the yard. If you can wait a minute or two till this rabble clears off I can find somewhere,' he answered. 'I'll just finish this horse.' He removed three straws from the horse's tail and gave it a perfunctory brush. Then he threw on a checked summer sheet, buckled it over the horse's chest, drew up the surcingle and, collecting his tools into a wooden box, he came out into the yard as the ponies clattered away down the road. 'I'll just see where we can talk,' he said, and disappeared round a corner. He returned a moment later. 'The saddle room's full of St. Trinian's girls and Mr. Goff's in the office, so we'll have to use the forage room, I'm afraid.' He led the way into a wooden lean-to building with a concrete floor. A row of corn bins stood along one wall. Squat sacks crowded together in a corner. Heath Robinson-looking machines—the oat crusher and chaff cutter—took on a mediaeval air, as they stood among the brightly-coloured paper sacks which held the modern horse nuts.

'Take a pew,' said Laurence Keswick, seating himself on a corn bin. Jackson, who had observed the white floury dust which covered everything, prudently leaned against the door post. Roper sat down on a bale of hay which awaited conversion into chaff.

For a moment or two Jackson stood looking at Keswick in silence. The man appeared good-humoured and relaxed. Apart from his height and the long face, which was well-proportioned and pleasant-looking, he did not resemble the dead woman at all. He had rough dark hair, very steady grey eyes, a straight nose and a slightly sardonic mouth.

'Full names?' asked Jackson suddenly.

'Laurence John Bartholomew Keswick,' Keswick answered, with a wry look at Roper, who had to write it down.

'You were related to Miss Thistleton?'

'Yes, she was my first cousin once removed; she and my mother were first cousins.'

'Did you know that you were chief beneficiary under her will?'

'Yes, I had a letter from the solicitors this morning.'

'Was that the first you knew about it?'

'It was the first time I knew for certain. My cousin actually announced that I was her heir on my twenty-first birthday, it caused a family row as my parents thought the expectation of so much money would ruin my character, but I never dared to count on it. For one thing at that time, sixteen or seventeen years ago, she might still have married and then she's always been rather a difficult person and very easy to quarrel with.'

'You were at the Upshott Show on Friday and Saturday, did you have any conversation with Miss Thistleton there?'

'No.'

'None at all?' Jackson sounded disbelieving.

Keswick said, 'Well, I suppose this has got to come out sooner or later, but the fact was that we were—well, that she was quarrelling with me. I'd had a letter from her on the Friday morning and I was waiting until I'd cooled off before I answered it and knowing what she's like—she never hesitated to speak her mind in the most public places—I thought I'd better keep away from her or we'd be having a slanging match in the middle of the show-ground.'

'Have you this letter?' asked Jackson.

'No,' Keswick answered, 'I tore it up.'

'Did she threaten to disinherit you?'

'Oh yes, very melodramatic, all the lot.'

'And it was over your marriage, I believe,' said Jackson.

For the first time during the interview Keswick looked uncomfortable. 'Yes,' he answered, 'you seem to know a lot about it.'

'Miss Thistleton disapproved of divorce, I take it, and thought she might dissuade you from contemplating such a step?' said Jackson.

'We-ll, she'd never shown any sign of holding strong views on the subject before. I think, myself, she liked to wield power, or she may just have been in a bad temper; she had very little control over her temper. Though I do think,' he added thoughtfully, 'that in her own way, which was far from demonstrative, she was fond of Marion—my wife—that might possibly have caused her to take sides.'

'So you hadn't answered Miss Thistleton's letter and you didn't speak to her between receiving it and her death,' said Jackson thoughtfully. 'Now, what about your wife—I imagine you had some conversation with her at the show?'

'No.' Keswick looked decidedly uncomfortable. 'I—er—raised a hand in greeting, but I don't think she saw me, that was all.'

'Have you communicated with her since you left home?'

'Sent her my address.'

'That's all?'

'Yes.'

'Did you go near Miss Thistleton's horse-box?'

'No.'

'Are you aware that the thermos containing the poisoned drink was in the horse-box under your wife's care all day?' Jackson's voice was loud and very hard.

'No, I wasn't aware of that.' Keswick raised his voice too. 'I thought the secretaries looked after that sort of thing.'

Abruptly Jackson changed his tone and the subject.

'You know Miss Christina Scott?' he asked, and when

Keswick agreed that he did, 'What sort of position did she hold in Miss Thistleton's establishment?'

'She rode for T.T. She jumped the horses at the shows for a fee and, I believe, a retainer; the same sort of arrangement as a jockey has. She would go over to Whittam and give them a school and sometimes she would train a young horse, but she never did any stable work or anything like that. She's what's called a professional in the show-jumping world, and she can't ride in the Olympics. The whole set-up's an anomaly though, because the rest of us are amateurs though we all depend on the prize money, and selling the odd horse on the side, to keep going.'

'Yes, I see. Now, Miss Thistleton seems to have made a change, on Saturday a boy called Brown was riding instead.'

'That's right. There seems to have been a dust-up; I've heard a lot of rumours about what happened but I don't actually know. Anyway T.T. changed her rider in the middle of a show, which is a fairly drastic thing to do.'

'And the Chesterfields?' asked Jackson. 'Do you know them?'

'Yes, well,' Keswick answered. 'Charity Chesterfield's rather a splendid person once you've penetrated her alarming exterior; her husband died about two years ago and since then she's brought up the children and coped with everything. Sarah, the daughter, is the one who jumps.'

'Now, do you intend staying here, Mr. Keswick? I shall have to get in touch with you again.'

'I haven't made any plans yet,' Keswick answered. 'As

I told you I only heard from the solicitors this morning. I've arranged to go to London tomorrow to meet them and the executors; the main problem at the moment is the horses—both my cousin's and my own.'

'Well, as soon as you decide on a course of action perhaps you'd let me know. Just telephone the Hamberley Police Station and leave a message for me, Detective-Superintendent Jackson.'

When Jackson and Roper rang the ship's bell in the thatched porch at Paddock Cottage, Christina Scott had just come in from exercising her one sound youngster. Dressed in blue jeans and a red and white checked shirt, she opened the door to the detectives and, on learning who they were, she invited them in.

Jackson had to bend almost double to enter the low-beamed sitting-room and when he raised his head he found himself muffled in chintz. The small windows were heavily curtained and pelmeted, the chairs wore flounces down to their feet, the cushions were frilled; observing brass knick-knacks, glossy magazines and no space left in which to put things down, Jackson denounced it to himself as a woman's room and gingerly lowered himself into the largest and plainest of the armchairs.

'Full names?' he asked, while Roper was still searching his pockets for his pen.

'Christina Mabel Scott,' she answered briskly.

'Now, Miss Scott, I understand that until last Friday you rode for the late Miss Thistleton?'

'Yes, that's so and on Friday we decided—well—to go

our own ways, for the moment anyway.'

'What brought that about?' asked Jackson.

'Well, Miss Thistleton wasn't satisfied with the way the horses were going; nor was I, for that matter,' she laughed. It was a hard, scornful little laugh. 'But we couldn't agree on a remedy. She wasn't prepared to accept my suggestions and I wasn't prepared to take all the blame. So it seemed best to part.'

'Surely it was rather drastic to make a change like that in the middle of the show?' asked Jackson.

'Well, Miss Thistleton, or T.T. as she was known in the show-jumping world, was like that. I mean if she'd asked me to go on for a day or two I would have done so—for the sake of the horses—but she didn't.' Christina made a gesticulation of despair with her hands. 'What could I do?'

'Mr. Keswick seemed to have heard rumours of a quarrel between you and his cousin,' said Jackson.

'I don't know how Laurence Keswick has the face to talk about rumours considering what's flying round about him.' Christina spoke energetically and her dark eyes were angry. 'And three parts of it true. At least he might arrange things better so's not to have two of his women at the same show.'

'Was that at Upshott?' asked Jackson.

'Yes, poor Marion Keswick looked as though she were on the verge of a breakdown and there was Laurence with that common little slut Helen Farrell hanging round his neck. She may be Lord Creech's daughter, but I still say she's a common little slut—three husbands by the time she was thirty.' Christina looked at Jackson defiantly.

'Is she the cause of the break-up?' he asked.

'No, I don't think so. She's been abroad and she's only just come back now that she's got her divorce; looking for husband number four, I suppose.' Christina laughed. 'No,' she went on, becoming serious again, 'the Keswicks have been breaking up for a long time. It was money with them. Laurence wanted to show jump. Well, if a man wants to show jump and keep a family he's either got to have plenty of money, be in the army or turn pro. Laurence came out of the army, bought a rotten little smallholding and tried to make a living out of that and show-jumping. Of course he failed. Marion's put up with it for a long time. Now, of course, they've a quarter of a million, but I think it's too late. Helen Farrell will use every trick she's got to hook Laurence—she's a proper little gold-digger—I don't think Marion stands a chance.'

Christina Scott hadn't known Helen Farrell's address but Jackson sent Roper to ring the secretary of the Upshott Show, while he recovered from the strain of interviewing Christina over a pint of ale. The show secretary told Roper that the address she gave them was of her father's London house, but it was common knowledge she was staying at the George Hotel at Hamberley, for what purpose he wouldn't like to say.

Jackson received this news with pleasure. He had expected to find himself trekking half across England, for how could you ask another police force to find out the things he needed to know about Helen Farrell? But the George with its dark Victorian panelling, its coaching prints, faded red carpets and warm beer was a favourite haunt of his.

'We'll see her at two,' he told Roper.

Helen Farrell, her thick, shining golden hair hanging almost all over her face, which apart from vast quantities of eye shadow was practically devoid of make-up, was so delighted by the notoriety of a visit from the police that she wanted to be interviewed in the public lounge bar. Jackson refused stiffly. He was far from amused by the knowing winks and grins he was already receiving from Stan the barman and, very conscious that he had a reputation to keep up in his home town, he hurried Helen Farrell upstairs and, finding the residents' T.V. lounge uninhabited for once, he bustled her and Roper inside and locked the door.

'Now, Mrs. Farrell,' he said, averting his eyes from the body-clinging green silk shirt and the pale yellow pants, which were the tightest he'd ever seen, 'your full names, please,' and he pulled violently at his nose.

Helen turned the lovely child-like face with eager gaze and half-parted lips upon him and answered, 'Helen Mary Alexandra Elizabeth Lomax Farrell.'

Jackson allowed Roper a few moments to write this down before he asked, 'You knew Miss Thistleton?'

'Yes, she was a horrible old woman, mean, disagreeable and always bullying those dreary secretaries,' answered Helen with energetic candour. 'I'm sure there were dozens of people *queuing up* to murder her.'

'Really, Mrs. Farrell.' Jackson was frankly shocked. 'You shouldn't say things like that.'

'Why not?' asked Helen innocently. 'I thought you were supposed to tell the truth to the police. I asked Laurence—Mr. Keswick—what to say if you came to see me and he said tell the truth, the whole truth and nothing but the truth.'

'Well yes, but—oh well, never mind.' He looked angrily at Roper, but there was a suitably shocked expression on the constable's pink and white face and no suspicion of a grin. 'Anyway, you were at the Upshott Show on Friday and Saturday; did you speak to Miss Thistleton at all?'

'No, you could see she was in a stinking mood a mile off; she always was if her horses didn't win. Actually I'm surprised that *she* didn't murder Christina Scott—she looked as though she'd like to.'

'Why should she murder Miss Scott?' asked Jackson stiffly.

'Because Christina wouldn't let those wretched horses jump. She was hanging on to their heads for grim death. I never thought her particularly brilliant even in her hey-day, but honestly on Friday she looked like pony rides on the beach. I'd heard she'd gone to pieces but when I saw her I wasn't at all surprised that she's been having such crashing falls and that all the horses were stopping. Of course she's getting on, she must be thirty-five.'

'Right, that's Friday; now on Saturday—'

'Oh, Saturday that ghastly Brown boy jumped them. He's enough to make you sick; I can't think why the B.S.J.A. doesn't ban him. And I can't imagine why T.T. asked him to ride her horses unless it was to humiliate

Christina; they had a flaming row, you know.'

'Did you overhear the quarrel?' asked Jackson sternly.

'No, but everybody seems to know about it.'

'I only want first-hand information, Mrs. Farrell. Now, still on Saturday, did Mr. Keswick spend much time with you?'

The ingenuousness of Helen's expression faded a little as she considered her reply. 'All his spare time,' she answered, 'but there wasn't a great deal of it. You know how it is at shows, you're for ever boxing and unboxing the animals, fiddling about with tack and studs and bandages; we were kept busy, especially Laurence, who was coping with two horses on his own. I had persuaded a girl I know to come with me and act as groom.'

'Did you go near Miss Thistleton's horse-box?'

'No. You see Marion Keswick, Laurence's wife, was there helping with T.T.'s horses and when you're on the loose again, like I am now, you're never exactly popular with your girl friends. As soon as they see you coming they all snatch up their husbands and run. Not that Marion could snatch up hers since they've already parted, but she looked as though she'd like to, so I avoided her.'

'Did you know of the existence of this "emergency basket" that Miss Thistleton had taken round with her?'

'No, I knew those dreary secretaries were always groaning under loads of stuff T.T. thought she might need, but I never bothered to find out exactly what it all was.'

'Right, Mrs. Farrell,' said Jackson with relief. 'That's all for now, but if you decide to leave the George would you let us know your next address in case we need to get in touch with you again? Just ring the Hamberley police station.'

Promising that she would, Helen saw them downstairs and then insisted on shaking them both warmly by the hand as she said goodbye in the lounge bar. Jackson observed with relief that Stan had gone off duty.

The detectives returned to the police station and having set Roper to deal with a backlog of small administrative matters, Jackson sat down heavily at his desk. Doodling on his blotting paper and sucking the last remnants of lunch from his teeth he pondered on the case. He was roused and revived by the afternoon cup of tea and went to collect Roper from the next-door office. 'We're going over to Whittam House again to have a chat with that Miss Hemming and a bit of a look round,' he explained.

The secretaries, relieved of their day-long attendance on T.T. and now recovered from that state of tiredness when simply to sit still is a pleasure, were finding each other hard to amuse. Led to the lawn by the sound of bickering voices the detectives found them sitting in deck chairs. Joy, knitting what she called a 'woollie' in pastel blue, looked pleased by the diversion, but Molly, overcome with embarrassment at having been caught in the act of repairing a brassiere, fled red-faced to the house, muttering incoherent excuses. Jackson, observing gratefully that her chair was the straight-backed sort, sat down in it and said, 'All right, Roper, you needn't take notes. I just want an unofficial chat with Miss Hemming. Now, Miss Hemming,' Jackson went on, trying to conceal his dislike by the heartiness of his voice, 'I suppose that living here with Miss Thistleton you must have seen a good deal of Mr. and Mrs. Keswick and as I want to get a true picture of how things stood between them, I thought you might be able to help me.'

'Well, I can't say I was in their confidence, Superintendent, but of course I'll help you if I can.'

'I've heard a lot of different stories, and I've talked to this Mrs. Farrell,' Jackson went on in tones of distaste, 'and I can't quite make out what to believe. Now what do you think the trouble was? Did Miss Thistleton know, being a relation?'

Joy Hemming knitted a few stitches thoughtfully and then laid down her needles. 'I think I can help you there,' she answered. 'One way and another we've seen quite a lot of them. Miss Thistleton always asked them to dinner regularly once a month and they almost always came; I suppose Laurence Keswick knew which side his bread was buttered because no one would have come for the conversation and certainly not the food. Then whenever T.T. bought a new horse she liked Laurence to come over and give his opinion. Not that she thought anything of his opinion, mind you, she was quite sure that she knew a great deal more about horses than he did.'

'And when did this trouble start between the Keswicks?' Jackson prompted her.

'Oh, it was only about a month ago that it became obvious to outsiders, I remember, it was the last time they came to dinner. Mrs. Maggs had excelled herself, we had white fish in a lumpy cheese sauce and Marion

Keswick nearly snapped Laurence's head off. We were very taken aback because they'd always seemed—well, rather a devoted couple before that.'

'And what did she snap his head off about?' asked Jackson wearily.

'Money.' Joy lowered her voice. 'It was all over money. I think that's partly why T.T. was so angry about it; she knew very well that it was in her power to help them, but she hated doing anything for anyone, so she wouldn't. Marion Keswick worked like a black on that little farm and did all the household work as well, but Laurence was always going off show-jumping; she used to go with him, but gradually she stayed at home more and more; she always seemed to have to pick the fruit or feed the pigs or something. I know, you see, because we went to so many of the same shows.'

'And you don't think,' said Jackson, heaving himself to his feet, 'that Mrs. Farrell had anything to do with it?'

'No, I'm sure she didn't; she's only just come on the scene.'

'Right, Miss Hemming. Roper.'

Brenda Dix, attired in a bikini top and the briefest of shorts, was sweeping the stable yard in a very languid manner; by turning her charges out to grass she had saved herself the trouble of grooming, exercising, mucking out and tack cleaning and she was concentrating on acquiring a suntan. One glance was enough for Jackson, who directed his gaze to the stable clock, which was five minutes slow, and asked stiffly, 'Where is the horse-box garaged, Miss Dix?'

'Hullo, you again!' cried Brenda Dix, flashing her smile at Roper. 'You want to see the horse-box, do you? Come along then.' The muck heap, a long open shed with wheelbarrows and a few jumps in it and the building which housed the horse-box were all discreetly hidden behind the red-brick Victorian stables.

'Here you are,' said Brenda. 'These two ramps are where the horses get in and out and this is the groom's compartment. Do you want to go inside?' She opened the door and as Jackson climbed inside she began to chatter to Roper.

There was nothing much to see; the box had evidently been swept out since Saturday. Jackson, visualizing all the saddles and bridles and rugs and buckets he had been told horses had to have, could see the groom's compartment would be full without the addition of T.T.'s miscellaneous collection. But the box was well fitted up, he thought, observing saddle brackets and plenty of hooks. On one hook a forgotten mackintosh still hung. Idly he took it down. He looked for a name inside and not finding one he felt in the pockets. He drew out a number of greyish-green fruits; some of the hulls were splitting to reveal almond-shaped kernels. He looked at them for a moment or two and then, quite suddenly, his mind identified them.

'Who does this mackintosh belong to?' he demanded. His voice was so sharp that Roper jumped to attention and Brenda gaped at him with horrified surprise.

'Oh, it's Mrs. Keswick's,' she said. 'It's been there since Saturday; she must have forgotten it, but with no chauffeur I couldn't send it back.'

'I'll take it with me,' said Jackson grimly. 'I shall be seeing her presently.'

Jackson dropped Roper in Hamberley, instructing him to find Sergeant Caley and get some tea as he'd be wanting them both presently, and drove on to the local nursery gardens whose proprietor he knew. When he returned to the police station there was a jubilant gleam in his small eyes.

'You two pop up and fetch Mrs. Keswick,' he told Caley and Roper. 'Say I want another word with her about Saturday.'

He then sent for some more tea and for Inspector Craker to whom he told, in depressingly unequivocal terms, exactly what he thought of the lack of progress in the arson case.

He had just finished with Craker when the telephone rang and Sergeant Caley's voice explained apologetically that they'd be a little time yet as Mrs. Keswick refused to come until she'd fed the dog and the pigs and the chickens.

'Well, hurry her up as much as you can, I want to get home tonight. And you mind she doesn't give you the slip; she's probably nipping off now while you're standing there talking to me,' Jackson began to shout as the thought occurred to him.

'I left Roper to keep an eye on her,' answered Caley defensively.

'Fat lot of good he'll be if she does make a run for it,' said Jackson, contemptuous but mollified. 'All right, Caley, bring her along as soon as you can.'

It was seven o'clock when Caley and Roper escorted

an obviously nervous Marion Keswick up to Jackson's office, and the note of doom in the Superintendent's voice as he said, 'Sit down, Mrs. Keswick, and tell me if this is your mackintosh?' did nothing to reassure her.

Marion looked at the mackintosh anxiously. 'Yes, I think so,' she answered.

'You're not sure?'

'Well, it's the same make and it's got a yellow lining.' She stood up and shook it out to examine it better. 'Yes, it's minus this button and there's the colic drench stain on the arm; yes, I'm sure it's mine. Where did you find it?'

'Never mind about that,' said Jackson. 'The point is what were these doing in the pocket?' and he produced the handful of greyish-green fruits.

'I can't imagine,' Marion looked at them nervously. 'I didn't put them there.'

'No? And I suppose you don't know what they are, either,' said Jackson with heavy sarcasm.

'No,' Marion agreed, 'I don't think I do.'

'Well, I'll tell you. They're almonds, bitter almonds, Mrs. Keswick. And do you know what they contain? No, I thought not,' he went on when Marion shook her head. 'Well, I'll tell you that too. Hydrocyanic acid—prussic acid if you like—the stuff that killed Miss Thistleton; the stuff that someone put in that thermos of milk shake.

'Now then, Mrs. Keswick,' he went on after a pause; 'perhaps you'd like to tell me what these almonds were doing in your mackintosh pocket?'

'I don't know,' Marion answered. 'I didn't put them there.' She sounded frightened.

'It's no use your lying to us; if you didn't put them there, then who did? It's your mackintosh, you said so yourself. And another thing, you told me you didn't touch that basket; we know that's a lie. We can prove you handled the thermos, Mrs. Keswick, it had your fingerprints on it.'

Seeing that Marion was completely crushed by this revelation Jackson opened the door and shouted for Roper to come and take down a statement. But taken backwards and forwards through her previous statement, confronted alternately with the almonds and the fact of the fingerprint on the thermos, Marion refused to admit that she had lied. She received Jackson's suggestion that she had poisoned T.T. so that Laurence might inherit, with horror and when he persisted in this theory she asked at last if he thought she would commit murder so that her husband could afford to go off with another woman, and subsided into tears. Revolted by the sight of tears Jackson told Caley to take over. But Caley's Latin charm, his cigarettes and cups of tea had no more effect on Marion than Jackson's noisy sarcasm. She hardly noticed when Jackson came back and sitting down wearily, began all over again with the almonds in her mackintosh pocket. Jackson was already looking for an escape from the situation when his telephone rang and the policewoman on the switchboard said, 'The Chief Fire Officer for you, sir.' Immediately Jackson's ear was assailed by a storm of words. 'What's that?' he demanded testily. The angry voice of the Chief Fire Officer became coherent. 'I said that the new Woolworths is on fire; it's gone up like a bloody paint store, which means it's arson again and what are you police doing? Bugger all!'

'Len, Len,' said Jackson urgently, but the infuriated fire officer had already slammed down his receiver. Jackson sat for a few moments staring straight in front of him, then, suddenly, he saw his way clear. With one stroke he would be rid of this obstinate, tearful woman, the horse-jumping gossips and bikini-clad girls.

'Mrs. Keswick,' he asked, 'have you a passport?' And when Marion admitted that she had, he went on, 'Well, Constable Grant will take you home now. I want you to give him your passport.' Taking Grant, who'd relieved Roper, on one side, he told him to stay at Down End Farm and see that Marion stayed there until further notice. When they had gone he gave a great sigh of relief and, picking up his telephone receiver, he dialled the Chief Constable's number. As he waited for Murray to answer, the look on his face was that of a man determined to have his own way.

CHAPTER FOUR

DETECTIVE Chief Inspector James Flecker had barely entered his office on Wednesday morning when he received a summons from the Assistant Commissioner.

Flecker took a guilty glance at his watch and mentally thanked God that he was on time, for Lestrange's violent views on punctuality were well-known and only the week before all hell had been loosed over the late arrival of a very newly promoted Detective Superintendent. A dark, dyspeptic man of tremendous drive and immense capabilities, the A.C. Crime was not generally popular in Central Office, but Flecker, who'd suffered more from the bureaucratic bumblings of his immediate superiors than from the A.C.'s inability to suffer fools, admired and rather liked him.

'Ah, something right up your street, Flecker,' said Lestrange cheerfully. 'Very macabre; hydrocyanic acid in the pink milk shake. Really, these horse lovers! I can't give you much information because I haven't got it. However, you'll be glad to know that the local people have the case "practically sewn up"—curious how often Chief Constables tell us that when they ask for help—but as some maniac is systematically burning down the town of Hamberley they've no time for the "loose ends". Well,' Lestrange looked up at him thoughtfully, 'no doubt you'll find out about that for yourself. You'd better take Browning and I should prefer, if possible, that you refrain from being burned in your beds.'

'Right, sir,' said Flecker briskly, 'asbestos sleeping suits will be worn.' He took the single typewritten sheet which the A.C. held out and turned to go.

'And don't be all night about it,' Lestrange called after him.

Detective-Sergeant Browning, whom Flecker found looking through a large pile of photographs of missing women, was delighted at the prospect of a trip out of town. 'Just the job,' he said, 'I'm browned off with this routine stuff; it's hard work, you know, trying to settle down after a holiday.'

'Oh yes, of course; North Devon, wasn't it?' asked Flecker. 'How did it go?'

'A really nice little place,' Browning told him. 'Quiet, you know, but good bathing. There was a beautiful beach, but of course the kiddies are too old for sand-castles; it's all flippers and snorkels and surf boards now. Mrs. Browning really enjoyed it; said she'd had a real rest.'

'Good,' said Flecker, 'and you don't look too bad on it yourself. Now don't take all day to pack. You won't need much and the A.C.'s in a hustling mood so we'd better bestir ourselves. I'll pick you up at your place in about an hour.'

Flecker whistled cheerfully between his teeth as he drove back to Kensington. Lestrange giving him this case was, he thought, like an answer to a prayer. For, to the pleasurable prospect of being his own master for a few days and the welcome escape from the dusty heat and tired, trampled appearance of late-summer London, was added an opportunity for success. He'd never bothered much about success before, he'd always prided himself on watching the rat race from the rails, but since, on his last murder case, he'd met Lesley Carlson, success which might lead to promotion had become very important to him.

He packed absentmindedly, and then, having arranged for his landlady to forward any letters—Lesley might write—he took the contents of his refrigerator down to the retired dressmaker who lived in the basement and was on the road again in twenty minutes. Browning wasn't ready but while he finished his packing Mrs. Browning entertained Flecker with tea, biscuits, photographs of the Devonshire holiday and Clifford's school report which, as usual, was exemplary. When Browning at last appeared, immaculately dressed in a lightweight suit, they stowed his large suitcase under the Chief Inspector's smaller one and Flecker, electing to drive, handed him the single sheet of information.

'At a horse show,' exclaimed Browning, taking up the sheet when he had finished directing Flecker along the quickest route back to the main road. 'Well, I never. Now if there's one thing I enjoy on the television it's the show-jumping. When they're televising from the White City or Wembley Mrs. Browning and I never miss a night if we can help it. Thistleton,' he added thoughtfully. 'No, I can't say I remember the name, but you don't take much notice of the owners' names, it's the riders and the horses you're interested in. The commentator tells you little bits about them all until you begin to feel you know them and that makes it all the more absorbing.'

'In fact you're an expert; couldn't be better,' said Flecker. 'Well, you know what you can do: there's nothing like gossip—'

'I'm going to enjoy this,' observed Browning, leaning back contentedly. 'Puts me in mind of the old pony I had when I was a boy. I never did any show-jumping; well, there wasn't anything like the amount of it that goes on nowadays, and in the summertime both the pony and I were kept busy on the farm, but hunting—he'd always get you there somehow, over or under or push his way through; you couldn't stop the old pony.'

Flecker said, 'I don't think, somehow, that you ought to admit to going *under* in show-jumping circles.'

'And what have you been up to? Have you heard any more from Mrs. Carlson?' Browning inquired with a sidelong glance at the Chief Inspector.

'Yes, she wrote last week. She's got a couple of free days towards the end of the month. Anthony's school goes back two days before the one where she's secretary. She's going to stay in London; I've put in for leave.'

'Very nice,' said Browning warmly, 'very nice indeed. We shall see you married yet.'

'No leaping to conclusions, *please,*' protested Flecker.

'Well, you want to take your time about it,' admitted Browning. 'What with losing her first husband and getting mixed up with that murder and young Barclay; and then there was the doctor,' he laughed reminiscently. 'I told you she wouldn't take *him*. She'll come round to it gradually though. Settling down, having a bit of home life and eating proper meals would do you the world of good.'

'I should get so fat they'd turf me out of the police,' said Flecker, trying to prevent the conversation from becoming serious. It was all very well for Browning to set himself up as a mentor on matrimonial matters, he thought, but he never faced the real problem of class. For though Flecker considered himself to belong to the new classless society in which manners, intelligence and the fact that you were educated were all that counted, he was well aware that Lesley's family with their public school and army traditions might not greet a grammar school educated policeman with open arms. A miner's grandson, thought Flecker, rubbing salt into the wound. Reared in a hideous little terraced house in a midland town by a forceful schoolteacher mother and a disillusioned and generally out of work father. Lesley was no snob, but she had her son to consider; Anthony was still young enough to believe that detectives were heroes, but later on—

'Hamberley,' observed Browning. 'Well, that didn't take long; I don't know what's happened to the road works this morning.'

Hamberley was a tidy town of no particular character, for the original Georgian buildings were now heavily outnumbered. Flecker drove down High Street, which had the disreputable look of a mouth that has lost a front tooth, for there was a ragged gap where the new Woolworths should have stood, and turned into Mason Street.

The County Police Headquarters had long been scheduled to move further out, but no large, cheap ancestral home having fallen vacant they had remained in the red-brick building between the modern telephone exchange and the Church of St. Luke and overflowed into an annexe behind. The police station stood sideways on to Mason Street and looked across its own gloomy courtyard, where Flecker parked the car, to the yellowish brick and grey slates of St. Luke's.

Flecker climbed out, stuffed the single sheet of information into his pocket and led the way up the steps.

'What you want,' said Browning, 'is a nice briefcase to carry your papers in.'

'Something else to leave in buses,' answered Flecker, and stopped at the inquiry desk to ask for the Chief Constable's office.

Murray and Jackson had heard of Flecker, they'd read one or two of his articles in the Police Journal and they remembered seeing a photograph of him in the national press, but they were disappointed when he came into the room; they had expected him to show more signs of success, to look more imposing. Small for a policeman with a stocky figure and an untidy profusion of dark hair, his clean-shaven face looked too amiable, his rather shapeless mouth too affable, for a man of consequence and it was easy to miss the intelligent gleam of his deepset dark blue eyes.

Murray, looking from Flecker to Browning as they introduced themselves, thought, as people always did, that he'd have put his money on the sergeant every time. For Browning, tall, soldierly and well-dressed with his Anthony Eden moustache and greying hair, seemed to emanate self-confidence. But reminding himself that they'd heard great things of the Chief Inspector, Murray shook him warmly by the hand.

'It doesn't seem a very complicated case,' he began as they all sat down. 'Jackson feels that he's on the right track, it's just a question of proof; isn't that right, Jackson?'

Though he agreed with Jackson, Murray didn't mean to assume any responsibility for the case. If Scotland Yard managed to unearth some new fact he intended to let the Superintendent bear any charge of maladroitness alone.

Jackson pulled his nose. 'It looks that way to me,' he said, opening a folder. 'This Mrs. Keswick had the thermos of milk shake in her care all day; her marriage was breaking up for lack of funds, her husband stood to inherit the best part of a quarter of a million on Miss Thistleton's death. And, on top of that, she was carrying bitter almonds about in her mackintosh pocket.'

'Yes, that's right, Jackson. You'd better give them the gen. Go ahead.' Murray spoke with patronizing approval.

Jackson told his story efficiently. Browning sighed and averted his eyes as Flecker made notes with the disreputable stump of a pencil on the backs of used envelopes. He'll never learn, thought Browning, and they'd think so much more of him if he had a nice propelling pencil and a proper notebook.

'Well, I have Mrs. Keswick's passport so I don't think she'll get far if she does try to run for it.' Jackson closed his folder and brought them up to date. 'The local man looked in on her this morning and she wasn't showing any signs of leaving then. Mr. Keswick phoned us just before you arrived to say that we shall find him at

Whittam House during the day, from lunchtime today onwards; he's moving his horses in with Miss Thistleton's. The inquest took place yesterday and the funeral's tomorrow afternoon at two thirty. Now, is there anything else?'

Flecker looked through his notes reflectively. 'These almonds,' he asked, 'have you sent them to the lab?'

'No, but as I told you I've had them identified by an experienced horticulturalist,' answered Jackson.

'Yes, I'm not disputing their identity,' said Flecker hastily. 'I just feel that we'd better make quite sure the right stuff comes out when they're brewed up and anyway it gives the lab boys something to do.'

'Of course they should be sent to the laboratory; I can't think why they weren't sent at once,' Murray broke in with a meanly triumphant glance at Jackson.

'Oh, there's no urgency about it,' said Flecker, returning to his notes. He looked at Jackson. 'You say that practically all the dismissed staff can be ruled out?'

'Yes, there are two more reports to come in, but the rest of them have produced perfectly satisfactory evidence of their whereabouts on both Friday and Saturday.'

'And you didn't find a large bottle of oil of bitter almonds in the kitchen cupboard?' Flecker asked with a grin. 'I gather it's used as a flavouring.'

'No,' answered Jackson. 'Mrs. Maggs is a very difficult person to interview, but I came to the conclusion that she had no reason to want Miss Thistleton's death, in fact it's done her out of a comfortable post. As for the contents of the milk shake I've already said the strawberry flavouring had a negative report and the ice cream and the milk were consumed without ill effects by the rest of the household.'

'Right,' said Flecker, getting to his feet. 'First of all I'd better see Mrs. Keswick; can you lend us a large-scale map of the district?'

Jackson nodded.

'Well, good luck.' Murray stood up too. 'Jackson will show you to your office and see about the map.'

Jackson led them, by a labyrinthine route, to an office from which he'd turned out two of his own inspectors and left them saying that he would send a map.

'Well, well, we are coming on,' remarked Browning. 'And a nice view of the churchyard too,' he added, looking out of the window.

Flecker sat down at one of the desks and began to go through Jackson's folder of information. Browning dealt with a police cadet who brought the map, a policewoman with two cups of tea and Superintendent Jackson, who reappeared to ask whether they would like rooms booked at the George or whether they had other plans. 'It's comfortable,' he explained. 'but it doesn't set out to be smart, like the Royal and the Queen's. I know the manager so I'll see you're not overcharged.'

'Just the job,' Browning answered him. 'You go ahead.' But Jackson suggested that they had better consult the Chief Inspector, so Browning turned to the immersed Flecker and inquired loudly, 'Stay at the George, sir? Superintendent Jackson can fix us up.'

'Mmm?' asked Flecker, without looking up. 'Oh yes, anywhere you like.'

'You haven't even drunk your nice cup of tea,' Browning pointed out reproachfully.

When Flecker came to the end of Jackson's report he jumped to his feet, announced 'We're off,' and having gulped down his cold tea, he plunged out into the passage. Browning collected his hat and the map and catching up with his superior, who had already lost his way, he endeavoured to shepherd him through the rabbit warren of cream and green passages down to the street.

After her ordeal at the police station Marion Keswick had gone to bed but, despite four aspirins, her mind had turned in weary and unrewarding circles until dawn. Then she had fallen into an exhausted sleep and had only wakened at ten o'clock when the ugly, anxious face of the white bull terrier had been thrust into her own. She had dressed hastily and had toiled round the smallholding with buckets of food for the indignant pigs and poultry, before she again let the horror of her situation crowd in upon her.

When the disconsolate Matilda welcomed Flecker and Browning at the open front door, Marion was sitting in the sitting-room, huddled as though cold in one of the armchairs. She answered their knock and when Flecker had explained that they were from Scotland Yard and had taken over from the County Police, she pushed back her limp pale hair from her exhausted-looking face and asked, 'Do you want to come in?'

'Yes, please,' answered Flecker.

The dust in the sitting-room had grown thicker, the white hairs on the hearth rug more numerous, a few flowers in a jug on the writing desk had dropped their petals and withered unnoticed.

Browning began to make friends with the bull terrier; squatting on the floor he pulled her ears and addressed her cheerfully. 'Now this is what I call a real dog, madam,' he announced approvingly. 'She'd be some use as a watchdog; not like all these little poodles and pekes.'

Marion pulled herself together with an obvious effort. 'Yes,' she said, 'Tilda never objects to legitimate visitors and she's very fond of the postman and the baker and, apparently, the police, but she can be quite fierce if she suspects anyone of evil intentions—'

Flecker, observing that Marion was swaying on her feet, said, 'Shall we sit down?' And then fixing her with a stern eye he asked, 'Mrs. Keswick, did you have any breakfast this morning?'

'No.' Marion looked surprised. 'No, I overslept and then I didn't feel like it.'

'Really, madam, you'll be making yourself ill,' said Browning disapprovingly. 'Shall I make some tea, sir?'

'Yes, it might be an idea,' answered Flecker.

'But I'm perfectly all right,' Marion protested as Browning left the room, and, struggling to her feet, 'Well, if I've *got* to have some tea, I'll make it.'

'You answer the Chief Inspector's questions, madam,' said Browning, shutting the door behind him.

'But he'll never find the tea, or the milk or anything,' wailed Marion.

'Yes, he will,' Flecker told her. 'Locating milk is nothing to a detective and if he can't find it he'll soon come back and ask. He's quite all right, really,' he added, when he saw that Marion was still fussing. 'He loves making tea and his wife's so competent that he never gets a chance at home.' He produced his envelopes, tugged rather distractedly at his hair and said, 'Now look, Mrs. Keswick, you must try to help us. First of all there are these wretched almonds; if you didn't put them in your mackintosh pocket, we've got to try to find out who did.'

Marion's hands clenched in her lap and a mulish look came over her drained face. Flecker said, 'Presumably you didn't wear the mackintosh on the day of the show because it didn't rain, so we don't know whether they were there then or not. You see, if the murderer nipped into the horse-box and doctored the milk shake while you and Miss Dix were in the collecting ring, he or she could have put any spare almonds into your mackintosh pocket at the same time. Can you remember when you last wore it?'

'Not really.' She drew a hand across her face. 'It hadn't rained for ages, had it? I only took it to the show because the forecast said there might be thunder.'

'Where does it live normally?' asked Flecker.

'On a peg in the passage by the back door.'

'And you didn't leave it anywhere else before the show and you haven't loaned it to anyone lately?'

'No, not that I can remember.'

'All right. Well now, this emergency basket with the thermos inside. Have you any ideas about how you came to handle it?' he asked quietly.

Marion put a hand over her eyes. It's rather late to start remembering now, isn't it?' she asked.

'Not if you *do* remember touching it,' he answered.

'I think I do. I can't be certain though. It may be that I've tried so hard to remember that my subconscious has just obliged. I've a dim recollection of hurling things about in one of the panics you get into at shows when the horse should be in the collecting ring and something is lost. I seem to remember that that beastly emergency basket wasn't properly fastened, things began to fall out and I just shoved them back and shut it.'

'Well, that's a help,' said Flecker encouragingly. 'And you didn't see anyone but the secretaries and Miss Dix and perhaps the Browns enter the horse-box all day?'

'I didn't see the Browns go in,' Marion answered dully. 'Only the secretaries and Brenda.'

'The horse-box was in a park, I gather, with other horse-boxes all round it; can you remember the people in the adjacent horse-boxes; did you know them by name?'

'Yes, they were all locals,' Marion looked at him desperately, 'but you see I've got Friday and Saturday hopelessly muddled up; I can't remember who was where when.'

'All right, it doesn't matter,' said Flecker as Browning came in proudly bearing a tray, neatly set out with tea and biscuits.

'Sugar, madam?' and 'Will you have a cup, sir?' asked Browning, pouring out.

'Have you any friends or relations in the neighbourhood you could stay with, Mrs. Keswick?' asked Flecker, when Marion had drunk and looked a little revived.

'The Chesterfields asked me to go over there,' she answered, 'but I can't; there are the pigs and chickens to look after, not to mention the dog.'

'You could take the dog with you,' Flecker told her. 'And who normally feeds the rest of the livestock?'

'My husband or I.'

'Well, Mr. Keswick can come up and feed them then,' said Flecker. 'If you like I'll get hold of him and tell him so.'

'You might not be able to find him or he may not be able to come or something,' objected Marion weakly.

'I can certainly find him; I shall be seeing him this afternoon, and if he can't come up himself he must arrange for someone else to do it,' Flecker told her belligerently. 'Go and telephone your friends and tell them you're coming after all,' he added, 'otherwise I shall import a policewoman to keep you company.'

'Quite right too,' said Browning as Marion went out to the hall. 'She hardly knows what she's doing.'

When the visit was arranged they waited for Marion to pack. Flecker sat in the sitting-room doodling and drawing tiny gibbets on the folder which contained Jackson's report, while Browning bustled round washing up cups, shutting the downstairs windows and turning off the electricity at the main switch. When she re appeared, carrying a suitcase and still protesting weakly, they put her and the dog in the back of the car and drove them firmly to Frailford.

About four miles from Whittam, Frailford was in a more truly agricultural area, with large, flat, elm-bound fields. The Chesterfield house, square and white with wide sash windows, had been a farmhouse, but was now divested of most of its land. White doves cooed from an outhouse roof and the whole atmosphere was rural and peaceful and comfortably shabby. As the car stopped Charity Chesterfield came hurrying down the flagged path to the garden gate. A small, square figure wearing bright blue jeans and a green blouse, she welcomed Marion volubly.

'You look all in, you silly girl. Why didn't you come before? You know we wanted to have you. Sarah, take 'Tilda and don't let her eat the cairns. Hughie,' she shouted, 'come and take Marion's suitcase.' She turned back to the detectives. 'Thank goodness someone had some sense; I'll look after her.'

Flecker said, 'Thank you, and we'll come and see her tomorrow morning if we may.'

'And you won't forget about the animals, will you?' pleaded Marion as she was led away up the path.

'Don't worry, madam, I'll remind him,' Browning called after her.

They lunched, as it was growing late, at a lorry drivers' 'Pull in' on the main road. Flecker, coatless and preoccupied, wolfed his food, bacon, eggs and chips, followed by a tasteless fruit pie out of a packet, without noticing his surroundings. But Browning resented the ancient and discoloured oilcloth which covered the table, the smeared and drip-congealed ketchup bottle and the threadbare linoleum. 'Not much of a place,' he said sniffily as they went out into the sunshine.

'Oh well, they fed us,' said Flecker indifferently. 'And now for the erring husband.'

The stable yard at Whittam House was full of activity. Two Land Rovers and two trailers were parked on the gravel sweep in front of the red-brick stable block; hurrying figures carrying saddlery, hay nets and buckets darted about and from inside the stable came restive trampling noises and agitated whinnies.

'Looking for someone?' inquired Brenda Dix cheerfully as she scurried by with a hay net.

'Yes, Mr. Keswick,' answered Flecker, 'but there's no desperate hurry.' He'd already located a man whom he felt must be Keswick. He was wearing an open-neck shirt and drill trousers and was fully engaged in trying to placate a very hysterical horse.

Gradually calm prevailed and Keswick, warned of their presence by Brenda, came out to find the detectives sitting on the mounting block.

'Sorry about that,' he said. 'We've been having a bit of a shuffle round; the idea was to get the whole lot under one roof.'

'That's all right, we were quite happy sunning ourselves,' Flecker answered. 'I'm Chief Inspector Flecker and this is Sergeant Browning. We're from Scotland Yard.'

'Oh.' Keswick looked surprised. 'They've called you in, have they?'

'The County Police are busy with this fire raiser,' Flecker explained. 'I'm afraid I've a lot of questions to ask you, Mr. Keswick.'

Keswick scratched his head and looked round him uncertainly. 'Well, I suppose we can go up to the house,' he said. 'The secretaries ought to be able to find a corner for us somewhere.' He turned and yelled, 'Helen.'

Helen Farrell almost justified a departure from the

straight and narrow, thought Flecker. She was lovely to look at, she emanated sex and yet at the same time there was a cool, childlike and somehow innocent quality about her that was very appealing. He remembered Jackson's observation that she'd discarded three husbands before she was thirty.

Keswick said, 'Scotland Yard on the job, Helen.'

'Scotland Yard?' said Helen, and turned her limpid gaze on the detectives.

'Mrs. Farrell?' asked Flecker, and when she answered, 'Yes, that's me,' he added, 'I'd like a word with you too if I may, after I've talked to Mr. Keswick.'

'Come on then,' said Keswick. 'Brenda can keep an eye on the horses; we'll all go up to the house.'

The front door was open and Keswick led the way in; he was obviously rather diffident about using the house as though it belonged to him. He opened one or two doors cautiously and finally discovered Molly Steer in the morning-room.

'Scotland Yard is here, Molly,' he said. 'Can you spare the drawing-room for my interrogation?'

'Oh yes, of course, Mr. Keswick. Scotland Yard? You mean the police, oh dear. But would you rather have this room?' She began to gather papers frantically as the idea occurred to her. 'I can easily go somewhere else; it won't take me a moment to clear up,' she said in flustered tones as she scattered papers on the floor.

'No, we'd rather have the drawing-room.' Keswick shut the door. 'You'd better wait in the garden, hadn't you?' he asked Helen.

'O.K., but don't be too long, darling, or I shall come

and beat on the door.'

Keswick said, 'If you do that they'll have you up for obstructing the police in the course of their duty.' He sounded, Flecker thought, a little dry and withdrawn as though he felt the 'darling' had been a mistake.

The drawing-room was more formally furnished than the morning-room, with a depressingly sombre colour scheme of brown and green; the furniture was large, the hangings heavy. The room wore an air of opulence, not the gaudy richness of vulgarity nor the expensive elegance of taste, but more of a lavish mediocrity, a spending on dull and unbeautiful objects for spending's sake.

'Take a pew,' said Laurence Keswick.

Flecker sat down and produced his envelopes.

'First of all, we've persuaded your wife to leave Down End Farm and stay with Mrs. Chesterfield,' he told Keswick. 'She's taken the dog and I said I'd ask you to arrange for the pigs and poultry to be fed.'

Keswick looked embarrassed. 'Yes, I'll see to that. What's the matter with my wife? Is she ill?'

'I don't think she's a case for the doctor, but she seemed in rather poor shape,' Flecker answered, 'and I don't think she was bothering with meals.'

'That's typical,' said Keswick angrily.

'And of course she's not in a very happy position so far as this inquiry goes,' added Flecker a little grimly.

'And sitting up there all alone brooding over it is enough to give anyone a breakdown,' said Browning reproachfully. 'But I expect Mrs. Chesterfield will cheer her up; she seemed a cheerful soul.'

'If she doesn't send her right round the bend,' observed Keswick gloomily. 'Charity never stops talking.'

'Well, business,' said Flecker. 'Could you draw me a rough plan of the showground, with the horse-box park in detail so far as you can remember it? I want to know which horse-boxes were next to Miss Thistleton's.'

'I can try,' answered Keswick.

Flecker handed him Jackson's folder. 'Draw it on the back of that,' he said, and produced a disreputable pencil.

'On Saturday,' said Keswick, when he'd drawn in the main lines of the showground, 'my trailer was parked next to Mrs. Farrell's. We were in the same line as T.T.'s box, but about six nearer the entrance so far as I remember. The later arrivals parked behind us.' He drew them in. 'Of course most of the people in this park were fairly local,' he explained. 'As it was a two-day show they fixed up to use Brunswick's winter quarters for stabling—they're the local circus—and the field between the show-ground and the stables was a park for the caravans and the horse-boxes of the long-distance people; a lot of them live in their horse-boxes during the show season and so they were put nearer what are known as facilities—in other words water taps and lavatories.'

Flecker looked at the plan with interest. 'Who did the boxes and trailers next to Miss Thistleton's belong to?' he asked.

Keswick scratched his head. 'Brown's was somewhere near,' he said, and the Chesterfields and the Pratts and Potling, a local farmer and a load or two of Pony Club children who'd shared cattle trucks and were riding in the gymkhana. Oh yes, and the army had sent a contingent from Windsor. It's difficult to say exactly who was next door, but Brenda might know.'

'Thank you very much,' said Flecker, taking the folder. He looked through his envelopes. 'I gather you didn't talk to Miss Thistleton on either Friday or Saturday; when did you last speak to her?'

'About a couple of weeks ago,' Keswick answered. 'At Dexley, I think. That's right, she poured out all her woes to me in anger rather than sorrow. It was soon after Christina Scott hit this bad patch. T.T. hadn't won a prize for three or four shows and she was getting very worked up about it.'

'What made Miss Scott—er—lose her form?' asked Flecker. 'I imagine she normally won a good deal.'

'Yes, she's done very well in the past. She wasn't quite top class, but she's represented Britain abroad a good bit. T.T. wouldn't have taken her on without a winning record. I don't know what went wrong. She's had some pretty unpleasant falls just lately, but I don't think her trouble began with a crash. Of course for a lot of us our show-jumping technique is a sort of gift from God. We don't know exactly what we do and if we try to analyse it and then decide that by pulling this string and that string we'll jump a clear round every time, we generally go off form. A lot of show-jumping riders have never recovered from being trained or taking lessons in style. You've got to learn to ride before you start jumping and once you've begun to win the less you think about your technique the better. At least that's my opinion.'

'In fact you suspect that Miss Scott found herself in the

position of the centipede who learned that he had a hundred legs and then couldn't decide which one to move next?'

'Yes, that about it,' agreed Keswick.

Flecker looked through his notes. 'Did you know about this emergency basket?' he asked.

'I knew there was an object T.T. called her emergency basket which was taken to shows, but I didn't know it included thermoses of milk shake,' answered Keswick.

'That's the point,' said Flecker thoughtfully. 'I don't suppose that it was generally known that she carried round a thermos for her especial use. It rather limits us to her immediate circle. All right, Mr. Keswick,' he went on, getting to his feet, 'thank you very much for your help and would you send in Mrs. Farrell, please.'

As Keswick went out Flecker turned to Browning. 'Go and have a chat with that blonde bombshell down in the stables,' he said. 'See if she can tell you which horse-boxes were next to the Thistleton one on both Friday and Saturday. And remember you're a married man,' he added with a grin.

'God!' said Helen Farrell as she came into the drawing-room. 'God, what an awful house. The outside's bad enough—North Oxford Scottish baronial—but the inside's worse. Have you been to the loo? It's still got the original stained glass.'

'Another hundred years and it'll be preserved as an ancient monument,' Flecker told her, 'and the Americans will be bidding for the stained glass.'

'The whole place makes me shudder,' said Helen. 'The thought of those three women cooped up here. God! I'm only surprised T.T. didn't have a blood bath long ago; I should have taken a hatchet to the pair of them. It seems so extraordinary to live like this when you've a quarter of a million. When I think what I'd have done with it—'

'You wouldn't have had a quarter of a million for long then,' Flecker pointed out.

'You're absolutely right,' said Helen energetically, 'but I'd have lived; not just mouldered.'

Flecker said, 'Well, business. Sit down, Mrs. Farrell.' He produced his envelopes and Keswick's plan of the showground which he handed to her. 'There's your trailer next to Mr. Keswick's,' he explained, 'and this is Miss Thistleton's box. Does that look like the right layout for Saturday to you?'

Helen gave it a cursory glance. 'Yes, I think so,' she answered.

'Can you remember who owned any of the other boxes?' he asked. 'Do you know which belonged to the Pratts and the Browns and the Chesterfields?'

'No,' answered Helen without, thought Flecker, even trying to remember.

'You didn't speak to Miss Thistleton yourself,' he said trying another tack, 'did you see her talking to anyone else?'

'God! What time did I have to watch what she was doing?' inquired Helen explosively. 'I was riding; I had a horse to see to and I was trying to take an interest in what went on in the ring.'

'As far as I can make out you and Mr. Keswick wanted to steer clear of Miss Thistleton,' said Flecker mildly, 'and that generally means one observes the person rather closely. One says, “Oh lord, there she is talking to so-and-so” and one dodges round the back of the refreshment tent or takes some other defensive action.’

‘Yes, I suppose in a way that’s true,’ Helen admitted grudgingly, ‘but we didn’t go in the enclosure much, you see there was a beer tent near the collecting ring. We only went in the enclosure for lunch and the loo and at the end of the day when the beer tent ran out. T.T. did wander round the horse-boxes a bit. I remember thinking that it was odd for her to be alone; generally she didn’t move without a retinue of secretaries.’

‘Friday or Saturday?’ asked Flecker. ‘Morning or afternoon?’

‘Saturday morning,’ Helen answered after a moment’s reflection. ‘I was just having a practice jump before the Grade C.’

‘Right, thank you,’ said Flecker, getting up. ‘I’ll probably have some more questions for you in a day or two, but I gather you’re staying on at the George.’

‘Yes, until Sunday, anyway. There’s another show fairly near on Saturday. I’m stabling my horse here with Laurence’s so I shall be in and out.’

Flecker said, ‘Would you tell the secretaries I’d like to see them now?’

A few moments later Molly Steer’s flushed face appeared round the door. ‘Mrs. Farrell said, but I don’t know if it was a mistake or not, that you wanted to see us. We didn’t know whether you meant both at once or one at a time or which you wanted first—or anything.’

‘It doesn’t matter a bit,’ Flecker answered her. ‘Come in, Miss Steer, and sit down. There,’ he added, pointing, as Molly stood rent with indecision, her gaze roving uncertainly from chair to chair. 'Can you remember,' he asked, 'how Miss Thistleton spent Friday evening?'

Molly Steer sat bolt upright on the extreme edge of her chair. 'Oh dear, I've such a poor memory,' she moaned.

'It was very hot,' Flecker reminded her, 'and Miss Thistleton was in a bad temper; she'd dismissed Miss Scott.'

'Oh yes, she was in a dreadful mood.' Molly Steer's eyes bulged behind the green diamante-decorated spectacles as she recollected. 'So unkind, she scarcely gave us a moment to collect her things together. But one shouldn't speak ill of the dead. I wouldn't like you to think that—I mean—'

'You may as well be honest,' Flecker told her, 'and we've more or less gathered what sort of person Miss Thistleton was. Did you have dinner immediately you reached home?' he prompted her.

'Oh no, we always changed. Miss Thistleton was most particular. I don't mean into evening dress, of course, but into something, well, suitable.'

'And after dinner?'

'Joy got the Browns on the telephone and Miss Thistleton arranged for the son to ride instead of Christina Scott. Then I had to phone Mrs. Keswick and tell her.'

'And then?' asked Flecker.

Molly thought for a moment. 'Oh yes,' she cried with relief. 'Of course, Miss Thistleton sent us for the scrap-books. So unkind, she let us bring them all in here and then it turned out she only wanted the year before last's and we had to take all the others back.'

'What do the scrapbooks contain?' asked Flecker.

'Oh, they're really a sort of record of each year. We had to paste in photographs and Press cuttings, things like that; they were mostly to do with the horses.'

'Was she looking for some particular thing?' asked Flecker.

'Yes, and she found whatever it was, I think, because she suddenly became much better-tempered than she'd been all day.'

'I'd like to see this scrapbook,' said Flecker thoughtfully.

'Oh yes, of course, I'll fetch it at once, they live in the morning-room.' Molly leapt to her feet. 'I won't be a moment.'

'Wait a minute,' said Flecker, 'I'll come too. Save carting it about.'

Joy Hemming was reading a newspaper. 'Scotland Yard, I presume,' she said, taking off her reading spectacles as Flecker came in.

'Miss Hemming?' asked Flecker, and introduced himself.

Molly Steer was looking at the bottom shelf of the bookcase; she proceeded along the floor in a crouched position, making small agitated noises. Then, suddenly, springing to her feet, she cried in distraught tones, 'It's not there, Joy. The year before last's scrapbook is not in its place.' She looked wildly round the room. 'What can have happened to it?'

'I haven't a clue,' Joy retorted calmly, 'but what does it

matter now?'

'The Chief Inspector wants it.'

'Well, the Chief Inspector won't blow up if it's not immediately forthcoming,' Flecker told her.

'It's probably there,' observed Joy calmly as she made for the bookcase. 'Molly never can see an inch in front of her nose.' She bent down and checked the year on the back of each one of the twenty-one green volumes. 'No, she's right; it's not there. That's very peculiar.'

'Do either of you remember putting it back?' asked Flecker, and when the secretaries realised that neither of them had put the book away, the search was transferred to the drawing-room and later to the dining-room and to T.T.'s bedroom. When Browning reappeared he joined in with enthusiasm and soon had the secretaries hunting in a more methodical manner. Flecker, deciding that he would be more usefully employed elsewhere, wandered off to the kitchen. When thunderous knockings brought no answer he opened the door into the large, old-fashioned kitchen with its wooden table and dresser and then led on by the sound of a wireless blaring away at its maximum volume he found Mrs. Maggs sitting in a wicker chair in a small room off the kitchen. The wireless on a table beside her was draped in newspapers which were held in position by a seven-pound weight.

'Good afternoon,' shouted Flecker, trying to compete with a powerful North Country voice which was advising children on the care and feeding of captive newts. 'I'm a policeman.' He handed her his warrant card. She read it slowly, examined it carefully and then reached out to switch off the wireless.

'The other one took away the bottle,' she said into the sudden and blessed silence.

'Yes, that's right,' Flecker answered loudly.

'No, not for the night; he never brought it back at all,' said Mrs. Maggs indignantly.

Flecker sat down opposite her in the other wicker chair. He wrote on an envelope, 'I'm trying to find out who poisoned Miss Thistleton, have you any ideas?' and passed it across. Mrs. Maggs read it carefully. 'It was something she ate at the show, that's what it was. I never did fancy the food they gave you in tents.'

Flecker took another envelope and wrote, 'I'll look into that,' and 'Did Miss Thistleton take a milk shake to every show?'

'If she was going to be out all day she did,' Mrs. Maggs answered.

'Did she always drink it?' wrote Flecker and passed another envelope across.

'Yes, mostly she did. I've only had to pour it down the sink once or twice all summer. I'm sure I don't know why you're writing all this, though,' Mrs. Maggs sounded indignant, 'I'm not that deaf.'

'No, of course not,' Flecker agreed with unconvincing falseness, 'only we don't want to make any mistakes.'

'No, I never worked for a Miss Takes; it was a Miss Coombs I worked for; nearly twenty years.'

Flecker extricated himself from Mrs. Maggs' domain bawling his thanks and making gestures of good will and returned to find his search party in very low spirits; the secretaries were snapping at each other and even Browning's enthusiasm was flagging.

'Leave it,' Flecker told them. 'See what the daily women have to say tomorrow and then we'll think again. One of them may have put it away somewhere.'

Joy Hemming returned to her easy chair and her newspaper but as the detectives drove out of the gates the dutiful Molly began to search again, toiling from room to room opening drawers and cupboards to a noisy accompaniment of falling objects.

'Was Miss Dix any use?' asked Flecker as Browning drove towards Hamberley.

'She's very anxious to help, and she's got more sense than you'd think from her clothes,' Browning told him. 'They got to the show early both days and Mrs. Keswick parked the box as close up to the trees and the hedge as she could to give the horses a bit of shade. Friday they had a farmer called Potling on one side of them and Miss Scott's car on the other, with Chesterfield's trailer next along and Mrs. Pratt's box behind them. On Saturday they were right against the hedge with Browns' next to them and Pratts' and Chesterfields' in the row behind them and Keswick and Farrell both a bit further along, but in the same row.' He passed over his notebook. 'I've drawn a bit of a sketch if you want to have a look.'

CHAPTER FIVE

CHARITY CHESTERFIELD looked across the breakfast table at Hugh's fair head and thin face bent sulkily over his plate and controlled a desire to scream with exasperation. Of a naturally cheerful disposition herself, she had found it hard to be patient with the moodiness which had overtaken him these holidays and though she knew that adolescents pass through these phases and eventually emerge as quite reasonable people, it seemed to her an almost wanton waste of what could be a comparatively carefree time.

'If it's going to be wet you and Sarah might go to the cinema this afternoon,' she suggested. 'Marion and I will be at the funeral, but you could take yourselves on the bus.'

'I don't suppose there's anything worth seeing,' Hugh answered obstructively.

'Well, look in the local paper and find out.' Charity Chesterfield spoke sharply. 'And do try to be a bit more cheerful, Hugh. We're supposed to be cheering Marion up and at least she's got something to be miserable about.'

'Oh, leave me alone,' said Hugh savagely, and pushing back his chair abruptly he rushed out of the room, slamming the door behind him.

Charity's stout body sagged a little. Whatever one did it was never enough; people refused to be happy. There was Marion upstairs wilting like a broken flower after a storm, Hugh behaving in an utterly impossible manner; only Sarah, who was still young enough to be delighted by a deluge of rain that would soften the ground for jumping, had worn a smiling face. Perhaps I'm wrong, thought Charity, perhaps we aren't meant to be happy, but there is so much on earth and if one has two arms and two legs and eyes to see and ears to hear—what more do they want? She crossed the room to the window. The rain was falling so solidly that it was like looking through the side of an aquarium and in the aquarium, clutching mackintoshes about them as they hurried up the flagged path from the front gate, were the detectives. Charity Chesterfield ran to open her front door.

' "Safely, safely gathered in",' said Flecker, grinning cheerfully as he removed his mackintosh and allowed it to drip on the doormat.

'My word, what a downpour,' exclaimed Browning breathlessly. 'Still, it's needed.'

'Yes, it'll save me watering what's left of the garden, thank goodness,' agreed Charity.

'How's Mrs. Keswick?' asked Flecker.

'Not very bright.' Charity Chesterfield allowed her depression to show. 'I wish—well, I suppose I really wish that none of it had ever happened.' She led the way into the pleasantly shabby sitting-room. 'If only T.T. hadn't flaunted her power and her money about. She asked for this.'

'Did she tell you she intended leaving most of it to your children?' asked Flecker.

'Yes, and I told her not to be a stupid old woman,' said

Charity Chesterfield bluntly. 'She'd let Laurence grow up expecting to inherit, she couldn't just leave him high and dry and I told her so.'

'Did you convince her?'

'No, not then, but I might have done by today if she hadn't been poisoned. Of course she loathed Helen Farrell; she'd have gone to almost any length to prevent her having the spending of Thistleton money.'

'But why was she in such a rush to do anything?' asked Flecker. 'Why didn't she wait to see if Keswick married Mrs. Farrell before disinheriting him?'

'That wasn't Theodora's way; she liked violent action. Besides, she wasn't expecting to live for ever. She had an operation about two years ago for some sort of malignant tumour and, apparently, if it came back there wasn't much more they could do. I think she liked to feel that her affairs were in order just in case.'

'When did you have this conversation about her will?' asked Flecker.

'Last week. Two or three days before the show, I suppose.'

'And did she mention it at the show?'

'There wasn't much opportunity for private conversation; she just brought me up to date with her latest ideas. She was thinking of leaving something to Marion—Mrs. Keswick—then.'

'Had you known Miss Thistleton for a long time?' asked Flecker.

'About fourteen years; we came here soon after Sarah was born. Theodora had lived at Whittam all her life.'

'And the Keswicks?'

'I've known Laurence almost as long as Theodora. When he was in the army she always asked him to stay when he had any leave and then gave a series of very dull parties for him. When he married he used to bring Marion, but it's only since they came to live at Down End that I've got to know them well.'

'What's Mrs. Keswick like normally?' asked Flecker. 'Would you describe her as a nervous person?'

'No.' Charity sat down on the arm of the large, shabby sofa. 'She isn't nervous of dogs or horses or thunderstorms or burglars, but she's a sensitive person and she didn't have a very happy childhood; that always makes a difference.'

'You mean she's basically insecure?' asked Flecker.

'Yes, I suppose so. You see, her mother was an actress, quite a well-known one, but father had gone off and I gather life was a very hand to mouth affair. Marion was dragged about all over the place and she told me once that sometimes when the electricity was cut off, because they hadn't paid the bill, they cooked over a candle.'

Flecker said, 'Oh dear, and I suppose she thought she saw the same pattern repeating itself.'

Charity Chesterfield, suddenly realizing that she had been talking to the enemy and that, as usual, she'd said too much, tried to improve matters. 'You needn't run away with the idea that Marion poisoned T.T. though; she's the last person to commit a murder. And, anyway, Laurence being well-off isn't going to help *her*, is it?' she demanded aggressively.

'No, it doesn't look as though it is,' agreed Flecker mildly. 'Now, you were at this show on Friday,' he went on, as he produced his envelopes. 'Did you see Miss Thistleton talking earnestly to anyone?'

'No, I don't think so, but you see I was busy. Sarah was jumping. She did very well actually. She jumped off three times against those objectionable little Pratts and came third; otherwise they'd have swept the board.'

'The Pratts' horse-box was close to the Thistleton box,' observed Flecker. 'Why are they so objectionable?'

'Well, they're always winning,' complained Charity Chesterfield. 'They arrive at the local shows with a truckful of ponies and carry off all the prizes. They spoil the atmosphere; they're so determined to win they ride as though their lives depend on it. They push in Musical Chairs and you'd never find a Pratt admitting that she'd missed out a post in Bending. And the whole family looks as though it could do with a good wash, mother included.'

'In fact they lower the tone?' suggested Flecker with a grin.

'Oh, here's Marion,' exclaimed Charity as Marion Keswick appeared at the door with the bull terrier at her heels. 'I was just telling the Chief Inspector why the Pratts are so disliked, though I can't think why he should be interested.'

'Local colour,' said Flecker.

'The mums hate them because they win,' observed Marion. 'I'm always rather pleased when they do. After all,' she turned to Charity, 'if Sarah wins you all feel a nice warm glow for a day or two and Sarah buys Copperfield a new head-collar or something. But when the Pratts win it means a square meal or that they can pay the electricity bill.'

'Yes, I know that's true,' agreed Charity, 'but I wish they'd earn their keep some other way. It spoils what should be a pleasure.'

'I didn't know horse shows were a sort of free fight for next week's housekeeping money,' said Flecker thoughtfully.

'Well, I'll get out of your way.' Charity made for the door. 'Don't let them worry you, Marion.'

Flecker said, 'Sit down, Mrs. Keswick,' and then when the door had closed behind Charity he turned to Browning. 'I forgot to ask Mrs. Chesterfield to fill in her trailer's position on our map; see if you can find her.'

'Yes, sir,' Browning answered briskly, and taking the folder he went out in pursuit of Charity.

Flecker turned back to Marion. She was sitting very tense and still in her chair; she looked wan, with dark shadows under her eyes. He sat down opposite her, pushed back his unruly hair and said earnestly, 'Look, Mrs. Keswick, there's one thing I want to make quite plain. If you didn't add hydrocyanic acid to that thermos of milk shake you've absolutely no reason to worry. I know it's unpleasant to be suspected of murder, but eventually I shall find out who did it and then the whole thing will be cleared up.'

' "Cleared up" is a euphemism for someone being hanged, I suppose,' observed Marion coldly.

Flecker looked at her with interest. She wasn't, he decided, quite as crushed as she seemed. 'No, not hanged,' he answered, 'unless he or she has committed or means to commit another murder; gaoled for life, that's about fourteen years—it doesn't seem a very unreasonable expiation. You see,' he went on as Marion sat staring before her, 'everyone on the staff had just as much opportunity to poison the milk shake, but you seem to be the only one with a motive.'

'Yes,' said Marion in a voice that grated with pain, 'it's so likely that I should murder T.T. so that my husband can keep Helen Farrell in comfort.'

'No, of course you wouldn't,' Flecker agreed, 'but if money was the original difficulty and your husband had only begun to take an interest in Mrs. Farrell since you parted, you might have killed T.T. in the rather desperate hope that with the money position solved he'd come back to you.'

Marion covered her face with her hands. 'Well, I didn't,' she said in a muffled voice. 'It never occurred to me. And, anyway, I don't think that money *would* bring Laurence back.' She suddenly raised her head and looked at Flecker. 'Don't you see, the whole point is that Laurence doesn't think money's important and I do. He's quite happy to consider the lilies of the field or to wait for something to turn up. He doesn't lie awake at night wondering how we're going to pay the electricity bill or what we'll live on if the pigs are the wrong weight for the bacon factory. He thinks he'll win the Open Jumping at Upshott or his premium bond will come up and he turns over and goes to sleep. It's all very well, I suppose, for two grown-up people to live like that, but you can't subject children to it; it's not fair.' There was a faint note of hysteria in her voice.

Flecker said, 'Yes, I do see. But you haven't any

children, have you?'

'No.' Marion looked down and flushed faintly pink.

'Do you know anything about T.T.'s scrapbooks?' Flecker asked.

'I've seen them. T.T. regarded them as a monument to her life's work; she was inclined to produce them after dinner.'

'Were all the photographs of horses?'

'Not in the earlier books: then she was still interested in relations and picnics and dogs and cats, but in the last few years, since winning became the only thing which mattered to her, they were all of horses. Generally they were photographed wearing their rosettes or with T.T. standing beside them holding cups. Sometimes a competitor's number was pasted in if it had been particularly lucky and then there were newspaper cuttings and once she even had wads of prize money stuck in. Some show had taken the trouble to acquire new bank notes and do them up in cellophane packets—usually they just send you a cheque. T.T. thought the money looked so beautiful that she had it stuck in intact. It must have been rather bitter for the secretaries, when they're so underpaid.'

'In fact she was fairly eccentric,' observed Flecker. He got up. 'Well, thank you, Mrs. Keswick; you've been a great help. I must go and find my sergeant,' he added vaguely as he stuffed his envelopes into his pocket.

The rain had stopped and already the Chesterfield lawn looked appreciably greener. Since the house appeared to be empty but for Marion and himself, Flecker wandered out and found his way to the stable, a humble building of brick and flint opening on a yard of moss-grown cobbles. From there a sound of hammering led him to the garage where he found Browning beating a Jael-sized nail into a dilapidated jump stand, watched by Sarah Chesterfield, a fair, solidly-built girl with a plain but pleasant face, and her mother. Charity, who was sitting on an upturned box and nursing an enormous vegetable marrow, saw Flecker first.

'Here's the Chief Inspector,' she observed guiltily. And Sarah pleaded nervously with Browning, 'You must stop now. I expect I can finish it.' Browning looked up at Flecker. 'Won't be a sec, sir,' he remarked cheerily.

'There's no desperate hurry,' answered Flecker. He leaned against the garage wall and looked down at Charity. 'I don't think I upset Mrs. Keswick,' he told her.

'Thank heaven for that.' Charity spoke forcefully. 'The poor girl's had enough to put up with lately. Your sergeant's doing his good turn for the day too—mending Sarah's jump; he said you didn't need him.'

'That's right,' Flecker grinned. 'Sometimes one policeman seems less intimidating than two.'

'There you are,' Browning looked at his handiwork with triumph, 'and don't you go having a smashing time again.'

'But I didn't, honestly,' protested Sarah. 'It just disintegrated with old age.'

'Well, we all come to it in the end,' observed Browning, handing her the hammer.

'Did Mrs. Chesterfield have anything to add about horse-boxes?' asked Flecker as they walked back to the car.

'No, she's not the noticing sort, that's why we went out to see Sarah. *She* knew where everyone was parked. A nice straightforward girl that, not like her brother.'

'What's the matter with Hugh?' asked Flecker in preoccupied tones.

'Oh, *he* hadn't time to mend her jump for her, *he* had other things to do. Sounded as though he'd got a real chip on his shoulder. His mother said she didn't know what was the matter with him, but he'd been like it all the holidays. Where are we off to now?' Browning inquired as they reached the car.

'Whittam,' answered Flecker, 'to see if the scrapbook's turned up. You didn't notice anything unusual about Mrs. Chesterfield, did you?' he asked as Browning turned the car. 'I've an odd feeling that I've seen her somewhere before.'

Whittam House seemed deserted and though the stables appeared to house almost their full complement of horses there was no sign of any human life, until a crash and the sound of splintering wood, followed by raised voices, drew the detectives towards the jumping paddock. At the gate they met a sad procession returning to the stables. Brenda Dix led a limping horse and behind her came Helen Farrell holding a handkerchief to her face while Laurence Keswick carried her hunting cap and riding whip. With them were the secretaries and a dark, broad-shouldered woman wearing a boldly patterned floral dress.

'Mrs. Farrell's just had a fall,' explained Brenda Dix cheerfully.

'Slap through the triple,' Keswick elucidated further,

'and she's in for the most beautiful black eye.'

'And a lame horse,' added the dark woman in censorious tones.

Browning nudged Flecker. 'Miss Scott,' he said. 'I'd have known her anywhere.'

'Christ, I'm furious,' announced Helen Farrell, removing the handkerchief and revealing a rapidly closing left eye. 'Do I look absolutely hideous?'

'Monstrous,' Keswick told her, 'and it's going to get worse. You wait till it goes green.'

'That looks a nasty bruise, madam. Painful too; bathe it in plenty of cold water,' advised Browning, while Molly Steer, finding an ally, began to entreat Helen to go indoors and lie down.

'She doesn't deserve all this sympathy,' Keswick told them. 'She insisted on giving the horse a school, though we all told her the paddock was like a skating rink after the rain, and she wouldn't even bother with studs.'

'It was nothing to do with the going; it was your fault, you told me to take the triple faster,' Helen retaliated sharply, 'and if you're going to fall who wants to be trodden on by a horse wearing studs?'

As Christina Scott weighed in with some advice on a standing martingale, Flecker detached the secretaries from the rest of the party.

'Any news of the scrapbook?' he asked.

'Not a sign,' Joy Hemming shook her head. 'None of the dailies has seen it since Saturday morning. It was on the table in the drawing-room then.'

'We've searched and searched, we've turned the whole house upside down, but it's simply vanished into thin air,' cried Molly Steer excitably. 'Mr. Keswick says not to worry, but it is worrying; where can it have gone? Do you think the murderer took it?' she asked Flecker.

'It's possible, I suppose,' answered Flecker. 'I think I'd better have a look at one of the other volumes, so that I can get an idea of the sort of information it contained.'

'I'll fetch you one, I'll run at once; I won't be a moment.' Molly Steer began to scurry up the path towards the house, but Flecker called her back. 'There's no hurry about that,' he told her, 'and I've another question to ask you. I gather that normally Miss Thistleton took either one or both of you with her when she was walking about. Were you with her all day on Friday?'

'Friday.' Joy Hemming looked thoughtful. 'Yes, I think we were. One or the other of us all day; but on Saturday she went off by herself for quite a while. We were very glad to be left in the enclosure. Poor old Molly's feet were killing her.' She laughed, and Molly Steer, obviously discomfited, flushed red.

'If you'd let me get a word in edgeways, Joy, I might be able to help the Chief Inspector over Friday. I mean about T.T. going anywhere alone.' She flushed again as Joy Hemming laughed. 'I don't mean the Ladies' tent.' She turned to Flecker. 'It was after tea, at least I think it was after tea.' She struggled with indecision. 'It was when she went across to speak to Christina Scott. You remember, Joy, it was really your turn to go, but you wouldn't, so I went instead.'

'Don't bother the Chief Inspector with those childish turns,' said Joy whimsically. 'Really, Molly, they're too trivial and half the time you don't really know whose turn it is; you know what a scatterbrain you are.'

'It's much fairer to have turns,' observed Molly obstinately.

Flecker pushed back his hair. 'Miss Thistleton went across to speak to Miss Scott,' he said; he looked at Molly. 'You went with her?'

'Yes, all the way to the horse-boxes and then she was so unkind. She just dismissed me. "I don't want you," she said, "you'd better go back." '

'And did you go back?'

'Not straight away. I was hot and tired.' Molly looked embarrassed. 'I sat down for a little on the grass.'

Flecker looked at her with interest. 'You saw what Miss Thistleton did?'

'I didn't see her, but I could hear her speaking to Christina in a very unkind way, a very unpleasant way. Then she stopped speaking and I thought she was coming back.' Molly was scarlet in the face. 'I couldn't hurry away, you see, I mean, well, I'd taken my shoes off and they wouldn't go on again.'

Joy Hemming began to laugh. 'Caught in the act,' she said, 'that's just like Molly.'

'Go on, Miss Steer. What happened next?' asked Flecker.

'She didn't come back. She went on to the next row of horse-boxes and began talking to Mrs. Pratt. When I'd put my shoes on I went nearer to make sure and then I hurried back to the enclosure. She came back soon after me.'

'Mrs. Pratt,' said Flecker thoughtfully. 'From what I've

heard about her I wouldn't have thought she was a person who'd have appealed to T.T.'

'No, she didn't. T.T. disliked her intensely,' Joy told him. 'And for once she was being quite reasonable.'

Flecker turned back to Molly. 'You didn't hear what they were talking about?'

'No, I was too far away, but it didn't sound a very nice conversation. T.T. was still speaking very loudly in a sort of bullying, no, I mean in an accusing sort of voice.'

Flecker said, 'Well, that's most illuminating, Miss Steer. Thank you very much and if you wouldn't mind putting one of the scrapbooks in the car—it's at the front door—that'll save you coming back here.'

Keswick was waiting in the yard. 'Did you want to see me?' he asked.

'No, I don't think so, not unless you can explain the mystery of the missing scrapbook,' Flecker answered. 'But since she's here, I'll save the ratepayers' petrol and have a word with Miss Scott.'

Browning was already engaged in conversation with Christina.

'Of course you've never had another one like Guardsman,' he was saying as Flecker joined them. 'Must have broken your heart to part with him after all those years. I remember you jumping off against Fred Hall at the White City—must have been about '59, I suppose. My word, that was a night. The wall was over seven feet by the time you finished.'

'Yes, it was a wrench,' admitted Christina. 'But the offer was too good to refuse. I'd have been a fool to turn it down. I sold him to the Italians, of course, but they haven't been very lucky with him; he's been lame on and off ever since.'

'Here's the Chief Inspector.' Browning had observed that Flecker was hovering round; 'I expect he wants a word with you, madam.'

'Yes, he does,' said Flecker, producing his envelopes, 'but it won't take a minute. I gather that you were at the Upshott Show on Friday, but not Saturday and that your only conversation with Miss Thistleton was when she fired you, is that right?' he asked, looking at Christina's strong, determined face and her rather calculating dark eyes.

'Yes,' she answered stiffly, 'except that I was hardly an employee so I don't think that "fired" is the correct term. Let's say we agreed to go our own ways.'

'Just as you like,' Flecker yielded easily. 'Did you see Miss Thistleton in earnest conversation with anyone else?'

'No, but as she spent the day in the enclosure and I was in the thick of the fray, I was hardly in a position to know what she did.'

'I gather she spent some time talking to Mrs. Pratt after she'd—I mean, you'd agreed to go your own ways,' said Flecker controlling his desire to grin.

'That's funny.' Christina Scott became interested. 'Normally T.T. wouldn't have touched Betty Pratt with a barge pole. If there was one point on which T.T. and I saw eye to eye it was that people like the Pratts should be kept out of the ring. After all they don't allow just anyone to train racehorses. People like the Pratts are in show-jumping entirely for money and they haven't the smallest concept of sportsmanship.'

'I wonder what that conversation was about,' said Flecker thoughtfully.

'I can't imagine, unless it was a few remarks about the weather or the state of the ground,' suggested Christina. 'Of course Mrs. Pratt's the sort of person who thrusts herself on you, especially when she's had a drink or two. T.T. may have just replied.'

Browning was disappointed in Christina Scott. Over beer and the ready-sliced bread and processed cheese which they lunched off in a Whittam pub, he grumbled about the television commentator who'd led him astray. 'Always made out she was such a nice person,' he complained, 'and really she's as hard as nails—selling the old horse for all she could get. Not at all a pleasant personality and she didn't look half the girl out of her riding things.'

'Well, if you will believe in these packaged images,' observed Flecker. 'Nowadays we're all so violently iconoclastic so far as anyone connected with Church or State is concerned, but absolutely worthless pop singers and show jumpers and footballers are built up into little gods. It's a very odd state of affairs.'

'Well, I shall think twice before I believe him again,' said Browning, still indignantly pursuing his own train of thought.

'Your commentator didn't tell you anything about this depraved Mrs. Pratt, I suppose?' asked Flecker and, when Browning shook his head, 'Well, drink up, we'd better go and find out for ourselves.'

They found Brake Lane with difficulty. The half-dozen gimcrack villas and bungalows which lined it were the work of a local builder who'd hoped that Hamberley would develop in that direction. But Hamberley hadn't and the unmade-up lane grew yearly more potholed and rutted, while the shabby little urban houses seemed to look wistfully across the flat, wire-fenced fields, across the railway line, the allotments and the gravel pit where the urban district refuse was dumped, to the street lights and gasometers of the town.

Two Ways stood at the top of the lane and looked squalid among the genteel shabbiness of its neighbours. The gate sagged from its hinges and was fastened with string. The front garden, which was simply trodden earth, was inhabited by a number of scrawny chickens; a missing window pane had been replaced by a square of cardboard and the dingy, half-drawn curtains draggled unevenly because of absent rings and hooks.

When Browning's knocking on the warped and almost paintless front door brought no reply, the detectives made their way round the side of the house, where a collection of sheds from which ponies' heads appeared convinced them that they'd come to the right place. Then beyond, in a dusty paddock whose only herbage seemed to consist of nettles and ragwort, they saw a woman and three girls unloading cut grass from a horse-box and spreading it about the field to dry in the sun.

'Mrs. Pratt?' asked Flecker, observing the haggard face, the almost shoulder-length hair with its harsh and partly outgrown auburn tint and blue Alice band; and then looking from the washed-out remnant of an elegant evening blouse, which she wore with a limp cotton skirt, to a pair of disreputable white sandals from which emerged nail-varnished but dirty toes.

'Yes?' answered Mrs. Pratt in surly tones while the three pony-tailed girls, armed with pitchforks, gathered round in menacing attitudes.

'Detective Chief Inspector Flecker and Detective-Sergeant Browning from Scotland Yard,' explained Flecker hastily, feeling that they had been taken for bailiffs. 'We're investigating the death of Miss Thistleton.'

'Oh, is that all?' Mrs. Pratt gave an unexpected smile, revealing horribly neglected teeth and then, assuming the mincing tones of extreme gentility, she inquired, 'But why come to see me?'

'I believe that you and your family were at the Upshott Show on both Friday and Saturday and that you talked to Miss Thistleton,' explained Flecker, looking round at the three girls in their tattered and mostly buttonless blouses, grubby jeans rolled up above the knee and the most extraordinary assortment of once elegant but now broken shoes. He found the sullen ferocity in their dark eyes disconcerting and turned back to Mrs. Pratt.

'Such a dear old thing,' Mrs. Pratt was saying. 'Such a character. She always had a kind word for the girls; they loved her. Didn't you, girls?' she asked sharply. 'Yes, Mummy', they chorused in unenthusiastic obedience.

'You talked to Miss Thistleton late on Friday afternoon, I believe,' said Flecker. 'Can you remember what you talked about?'

'Yes, that's right. We had a little chat. Now let me see,

what was it about?' She cast round wildly for a subject. 'Oh yes,' she continued with relief, 'of course, dear old T.T. stopped to congratulate me on Liz's win on Top Ten in the Foxhunter. She said that she wished that Liz was just that much older and she could have taken her on instead of Christina Scott, who was really getting past it.'

'Go on, Mum, did she really? You never told us,' observed the smallest Pratt.

' 'Course she didn't, Mum's making it up.' Virginia dismissed the idea scornfully. 'Liz couldn't jump an open course—she's windy.'

'Better'n you, I could,' Liz turned on her sister shrilly. 'But I wouldn't 'ave jumped for bloody old T.T. anyway. Not if she'd asked me. She keeps telling you what to do—'er and them bloody secretaries. I've 'eard 'em.'

Mrs. Pratt laughed genteelly. 'Now girls, that'll do. Finish unloading the grass.' She turned to Flecker. 'The things they pick up at school nowadays. I think we'd better go indoors, it's quieter there.

'Of course my husband had a kink, he wouldn't live with me; he left me when the girls were quite tiny,' she explained as she led the way in through the back door. In the kitchen several chickens pecked about the floor, including one with a family of half grown chicks. Mrs. Pratt snatched up a grimy cloth, flapping it and, emitting weird and high-pitched shooing noises, she pursued the cackling poultry round the room, winkling them out from behind the boiler and under the sink with practised flicks of the cloth.

'Of course, as I was saying,' she went on rather breathlessly, as the last chick, half running, half flying, pursued the rest of its family across the back garden, 'my husband left me so the girls haven't had quite the upbringing I could wish. They need a father's firm hand. Mothers,' she added with a self-conscious little laugh, 'find it very hard to refuse anything. I'm afraid you've caught us at rather an untidy moment,' she continued talking rapidly. 'With the haymaking and the horse shows and the holidays I haven't had a moment for the house—but then as I say to the girls, you're only young once.'

Browning, who'd been looking round at the uncared-for house with an expression of intense disapproval, brightened up when he saw the small, square sitting-room, one wall of which was entirely covered in rosettes. 'My word, someone's been doing well,' he observed.

'Just the three girls,' explained Mrs. Pratt, 'but those don't include this year's, we've quite a box full to put up at the end of the season. What about a little drink?' she asked and she began to search among a collection of pathetically small and mostly empty gin bottles.

'Not while we're on duty, thank you very much,' answered Flecker and Browning, recollecting the state of the kitchen, decided not to suggest a cup of tea.

'Well, won't you sit down?' said Mrs. Pratt and then, patting back her dry, tangled hair she looked archly at Flecker and asked, 'What else can I tell you, Chief Inspector?'

Flecker asked if she knew of the emergency basket or of T.T.'s scrapbooks and whether she had seen anyone unexpected near the Thistleton horse-box and received only negative replies. Then he tried a different approach.

'I gathered from other witnesses that the conversation you had with Miss Thistleton on Friday afternoon was less amicable than you remember it,' he said mildly. 'In fact I'm told that it sounded remarkably like a row.'

Mrs. Pratt's arch manner vanished abruptly. 'Who told you that?' she demanded. 'That stuck-up prude Christina Scott, that's who it was. She'd say anything. I'm tolerant, but I can't stand hypocrites. Always trying to make out she's a lady when we all know her father was a butcher. She's no better than the rest of us, but from the airs she puts on you'd think she was God Almighty, and then, when she thinks no one's looking, you see her running back to her car for a nip of gin on the sly. She's the one who quarrelled with T.T. The old lady went for her over her riding.'

'Yes, we know about that,' said Flecker, 'but luckily for Miss Scott she wasn't at the show on Saturday, so we don't have to delve quite so deeply into her affairs.'

'She *was* at the show on Saturday,' Betty Pratt sounded venomous. 'She was wearing dark glasses and a navy blue dress, but I spotted her in the crowd. She was watching T.T.'s horses, and smiling all over her face each time young Billy Brown hit a fence.'

'Well, I told you that I didn't take to her,' said Browning as the car lurched down Brake Lane.

'Mmm?' asked Flecker absentmindedly. 'Oh, you mean Miss Scott. Yes, well we can't take her to task now, she'll be at the funeral.' He shuffled through his envelopes. 'I really don't see that the Browns can have come prepared to repay any sarcastic remarks with hydrocyanic acid.'

'No more do I. Who says they did?' asked Browning.

'No one; I'm trying to save the ratepayers' petrol by convincing myself that we needn't pay the Browns a visit at this stage anyhow. Oh come on, we'll go to Down End Farm and have a poke round.'

'One other thing,' said Browning as he carefully negotiated the ruts and potholes of Brake Lane. 'We don't seem to have your mackintosh.' Flecker turned and looked guiltily at the back seat. 'No,' he admitted, 'we haven't, I must have left it at the Chesterfields'; never mind, we can collect it tomorrow.'

'And suppose there's another downpour like the one we had this morning?' asked Browning reproachfully.

'Oh well,' answered Flecker, losing interest, 'I shall just have to get wet.'

At Down End Farm Browning, having been briefed to look for any brewing apparatus or suspicious bottles, departed on a systematic search of the piggeries and chicken houses, while Flecker wandered through the deserted stables and the tack-denuded saddle-room. He found nothing but half-empty bottles of horse remedies which smelt very much as he expected horse remedies to smell, and then collecting a broom and shovel he went across to the house. He stood looking at it, wondering whether anxiety over a dwindling bank balance and growing unhappiness were all that had gone on there; or whether in that little red box of a house, the small element of free choice which is allowed us in life had been snatched at and used for impulsive evil or perhaps for a more sinister and premeditated plan. He sighed and made for the back door, reminding himself that owing to bonfires and compost heaps, country dustbins were generally less repulsive than town ones.

The Keswick dustbin was only half full. Flecker tipped the contents out and found among the eggshells and empty spaghetti tins—evidence of Marion's frugal living—a large metal object wrapped in newspaper.

'What have you got there?' asked Browning, joining him.

'Some sort of saucepan,' answered Flecker as a large double boiler emerged from the newspaper. The two men stood looking at it doubtfully. Flecker removed one of the small brown grains which adhered to the inside of the pot.

'Linseed,' Browning told him. 'You cook it up and feed it to horses; it makes their coats shine.'

'Well, let's see if it leaks,' said Flecker, advancing on the water-butt which was brimming with water after the rain. He filled both halves of the double boiler and held them out one in either hand. Browning bent down and inspected them carefully. 'Not a drop,' he said, when a couple of minutes had passed. 'Now what did she throw that away for?'

Flecker tipped out the water, reunited the two halves and handed the pot to Browning. 'Stick it in the car, please,' he said and turned back to the scattered contents of the dustbin. He was just shovelling in the last shovelful of garbage when Browning reappeared round the corner of the house, coughed warningly and announced, 'Here's Mr. Keswick, sir.'

Laurence Keswick was wearing a dark suit and black tie and he carried a suitcase. His long face was cold and hard with anger. He put the suitcase down beside the dustbin.

'I thought the Benign Father Figure or the Avuncular Attitude or whatever it was, was too good to be true,' he said disagreeably. 'I might have realised that all the concern about my wife was just a faked-up job to get the place empty so that you could have a good snoop round. "Poor Mrs. Keswick on the verge of a breakdown",' he mocked bitterly.

Flecker replaced the dustbin lid in silence. Keswick's remarks had angered him, but he recognized that the man was in a towering rage.

'Anyway don't you need a search warrant for this sort of thing?' asked Keswick, pointing at the dustbin.

'I can get a search warrant easily enough,' answered Flecker, 'but I'd still come and look in your dustbin, which is what you're really objecting to.' He pushed ineffectually at his hair. 'We can't get away from the fact that Miss Thistleton was murdered. It's my job to find the murderer and if that entails looking in dustbins I've got to do it. What's the point of my worrying Mrs. Keswick with it?'

'And why should my wife be worried because you look in our dustbin?' demanded Keswick aggressively.

'I don't know,' answered Flecker, 'except that she very obviously is worried by the whole case.'

Keswick was still slightly nonplussed by this remark when Flecker asked, 'When was the dustbin last emptied?'

Keswick thought. 'Monday,' he answered and then added with a schoolboy sneer, 'So you see you're too late. All those great bottles of prussic acid are already on the rural district rubbish dump.'

Flecker produced an envelope and made a note. 'Are you going to stay here?' he asked in equable tones.

'Yes, subject to police approval, of course,' Keswick answered sarcastically.

'You'll find the electricity turned off at the main switch beside the meter, sir,' Browning told him. 'When Mrs. Keswick left I thought it best to be on the safe side.'

'And took a quick look round the larder for prussic acid at the same time, I suppose,' observed Keswick scathingly. 'Another Judas-kiss.'

Flecker looked at him thoughtfully. 'Well, sir, we won't keep you,' he said in his most formal police tones. Browning took up the broom and shovel as Keswick, without another word, let himself into the house.

'Whew! He was in a temper and no mistake,' observed Browning as they climbed into the car.

'Did he see the cooking apparatus?' asked Flecker.

'No, I'd just put it away in the car when he drove up. Mind you, he wasn't in a very good humour from the first; you could see it wasn't going to take much to set him off.'

'Well, if he didn't see our cooking pot I don't think there's any need to rush into action,' Flecker decided thoughtfully. 'Back to Hamberley. We'll go through the gestures of using our office.'

'Just right for a nice cup of tea,' observed Browning cheerfully.

Flecker arranged the double boiler in the 'In' tray, his bundle of envelopes in the 'Out'. 'Not much to show for two days' work,' he observed, seating himself at the desk and picking up the telephone to ask if Superintendent Jackson could spare him a few minutes. Jackson could, and shaking off Browning, who wanted him to drink his tea first, Flecker set off through the labyrinthine passages. Jackson was surprised by his request for a good veterinary surgeon who specialized in horses.

'The local firm has a very good name,' he said, pulling his nose gently. 'Mr. Frogmorton himself deals with horses, I believe, at any rate he was down as honorary veterinary surgeon at the Upshott Show.'

'We'll try him then,' decided Flecker. 'It's really a botanical query, but I think he's more likely to provide an off the cuff answer than our lab boys.'

Jackson pushed the telephone across the desk. 'Help yourself,' he said, and with a glance at a list of numbers, 'Hamberley 215.'

Frogmorton was eventually located at home. He had a slow, portly voice and he listened to Flecker's question, whether flax was one of the many cyanogenetic plants and, if so, whether it was possible to release hydrocyanic acid from its fruit—linseed—in silence.

'Funny you should ask that,' he replied. 'We had a case a few months ago—last season—well, in January, to be exact. A client of ours lost a horse through feeding badly prepared linseed. Yes, it contains cyanogenetic glycoside and a liberating enzyme which under certain conditions becomes active and releases hydrocyanic acid. The normal procedure when preparing linseed for a mash is to boil it for at least ten minutes, this destroys the releasing enzyme. This client of ours put the linseed on to cook, but apparently the fire must have gone out underneath it, without anyone realizing it, and the stuff just soaked in warm water. Next day they fed the pony a substantial dose of prussic acid and that was that.'

'That's most enlightening,' said Flecker. 'If it's not professionally unethical can you tell me the client's name?'

'Yes, it was a woman called Pratt. Keeps a stable of jumping ponies which her daughters ride. They're a pretty shiftless lot, but this wasn't altogether their fault. It's not generally known that, given certain circumstances, linseed can become poisonous.'

'You mean that horse people generally don't know about it?' asked Flecker.

'A lot of them don't. But the ones round here do now; I've seen to that. I didn't want it happening again.'

'You've explained it to all the horse owners in the neighbourhood as you have to me?' asked Flecker.

'Yes, that's about it.'

'To the Keswicks and the Chesterfields and Miss Scott?'

'Yes, they're all clients of ours. I don't think we've missed out any of the locals. Most of 'em have probably been told two or three times as I told my staff to make a point of mentioning it too.'

CHAPTER SIX

FLECKER had spent most of Thursday evening sitting in a secluded corner of the lounge bar with a pint of beer and a volume of Theodora Thistleton's scrapbook. Browning, having looked briefly through the endless photographs of horses jumping, horses held by T.T.—tall, gaunt and unsmiling—bored horses waiting, while Christina Scott leaned down to take a large cup from some dignitary, and groups of prize-winning horses smugly conscious of their rosettes, had grown tired of his Chief's silent preoccupation and had disappeared upstairs to watch television. Now, eating his way through a substantial breakfast, he complained bitterly of the inadequacies and inaccuracies of a crime film. Flecker, never at his best in the morning, replied vaguely until Browning, swallowing his last mouthful of tea, inquired what the plans for the day entailed.

'We're going to act in accordance with the popular police image,' Flecker answered. 'Tearing ourselves from our usual occupations of hounding motorists and kicking nuclear disarmers we're going to bully defenceless women; Mrs. Keswick about the double boiler and Miss Scott about her unconfessed visit to the Upshott Show.'

'Ah well, they've asked for it; they should have told the truth in the first place,' said Browning.

' "Sole judge of truth, in endless error hurled",' observed Flecker gloomily. 'Sometimes I wish I'd chosen a different profession.'

'Well, you're not the only one,' Browning announced cheerfully as he got to his feet. 'Still we have our good times—'

At Frailford Farm house, Hugh Chesterfield opened the front door and his already sullen face took on an expression of mingled apprehension and dislike when he saw who the callers were. Hearing that they wished to see Marion Keswick he showed them into the sitting-room, and, eyeing doubtfully the parcel which Browning carried, he said he would fetch her. Browning freed the double boiler from its brown paper and placed it on a table. Flecker wandered round the room looking at the books, mostly complete sets of the classics or Book Society choices. When Marion came in she was wearing her tussore-coloured slacks and an old shirt. She had blue paint on her hands and a smudge of it across her face. Flecker, watching her entrance from the far end of the room, felt certain that she had seen and recognized the double boiler, but she ignored its presence and began to talk with nervous rapidity. 'I decided that it was no use my sitting about being a blot so I've been helping Sarah with her jumps—painting the dragon's teeth.' She held up her hands. 'They say professional house painters never spill a drop on themselves so you can see how much of an amateur I am.'

Flecker came across to the table. He pointed to the double boiler. 'We found this in your dustbin; why did you throw it away?'

Marion looked at him defiantly. 'It leaks,' she answered.

'Oddly enough it doesn't,' he told her. 'We've tested it.

It doesn't leak at all.'

'I'm sure it does. It leaked all over the cooker and you know what it is with electricity. If you get the works wet the fuse blows and since the electricity people always put the fuse boxes in such inaccessible places—ours can only be reached by a left-handed giant—I didn't want that to happen so I slung the pot out. Anyway with no horses there wasn't much point in keeping it,' she added on second thoughts.

'Did you know that hydrocyanic or prussic acid could be released from linseed?' Flecker asked her.

'No.' Marion was white-faced but still defiant.

'Mr. Frogmorton is sure that he told you, but perhaps it was only your husband?'

'I'm equally sure that he didn't tell either of us,' answered Marion firmly.

'If you didn't know about the lethal potentialities of linseed why did you throw the double boiler away?' asked Flecker.

'Because it leaked,' she answered with desperate obstinacy.

'It does *not* leak.' Flecker's voice was coldly patient. 'Do you want me to give you a demonstration of its watertightness? I will if you like. Sergeant Browning and I filled both halves with water and *neither* of them leaked.'

'That's right, madam,' Browning added his testimony. 'We've examined them both most carefully.'

'Well, then, it must have boiled over on the cooker and that must have given me the impression that it leaked,' said Marion.

Flecker tugged at his hair in an exasperated gesture. 'I wish you'd try to help, Mrs. Keswick,' he said and then, when Marion turned her face away from him and remained obstinately silent, he added, 'Well, I'm no third degree merchant; if you won't help I shall have to go and find someone who will.' He turned for the door and then asked over his shoulder, 'Did you know that Miss Scott was at the show on Saturday?'

'Christina at the show? But she told Charity—' Marion paused, 'I expect I've got it all wrong.'

'No, I don't think you have.' Flecker grinned at her suddenly. 'I'm offering consolation; I didn't want you to think you were the only one telling the police whopping great lies.'

Charity Chesterfield was waiting in the hall, her broad, plain, cheerful face screwed into unaccustomed lines of apprehension and dismay. 'I couldn't help overhearing you. The door was open. But it couldn't be Marion, I'm sure it couldn't be. Somebody must be doing these things to make you suspect her.' The words came out disjointedly as though her mind was elsewhere.

'Did Mr. Frogmorton tell you about the lethal potentialities of linseed?' asked Flecker.

'Yes, but I didn't connect it with Theodora's death; I suppose because of the almonds that were in Marion's mackintosh.'

'Yes, quite,' said Flecker, opening the front door. 'Well, goodbye.' Browning, who was trying to return the double boiler to its wrappings, hurried after him.

'Oh dear, oh dear,' he said when he had stowed the boiler into the back of the car and taken the driving seat,

'I don't like the look of this at all. She's in it up to the neck and yet you can't exactly blame her; she's only trying to keep her husband and that's natural in a woman after all.'

'Two wrongs don't make a right,' observed Flecker primly as he scuffled among his envelopes. 'Or, in other words, you can't hope to preserve the sanctity of marriage by the mortal sin of murder. Come on, let's see what Miss Scott has to say for herself,' he added, stuffing the envelopes into a pocket.

They found Christina. Dressed in jeans, jodhpur boots, a short-sleeved shirt and with a scarf tied over her head, she was standing in her small, neat stable-yard watching her girl groom direct a jet of cold water from a hose-pipe down the foreleg of a very resigned-looking horse.

'What have you got there,' asked Browning, 'a bit of a sprain?'

'No, he's throwing a splint; it's quite maddening. We've had one thing after another with him the whole season. I had expected to win the Foxhunter at Upshott with him and then this cropped up.'

'And Miss Elizabeth Pratt triumphed instead,' observed Flecker.

'Yes. And she won again next time out at Grinley,' said Christina. 'I don't know where Mrs. Pratt picked up that little horse, but for the sort of price she generally pays she got hold of a really good one. Anything with a pop in it costs at least three hundred pounds and I wouldn't have thought you'd find a good novice like that under six or seven hundred. And you're not going to tell me that the Pratts have a third of that in the bank; she can't have—she owes money all over the place. Of course I daresay his legs are a bit suspect; I hear that they had to withdraw him from the Grade C on the Saturday at Upshott, but it can't have been much for he was as right as rain at Grinley.'

'A mystery in fact,' said Flecker, producing his envelopes and making a note. 'I really came to ask you where you were on Saturday, Miss Scott?'

'Here,' answered Christina without hesitation. 'I spent the day at home.'

'Alone?'

'Yes.'

'That's tiresome. Can you think of anyone who called or telephoned or exchanged information on the weather over the gate?'

'No, I don't remember anyone coming.'

'What about tradesmen delivering? Baker, butcher, greengrocer? Saturday's usually a busy day.'

'Normally I'm at a show on Saturdays, so we've got all the arrangements cut and dried, if I do want anything left it's put in one of the containers in the back porch. On Saturday the baker did call, but I didn't speak to him.'

'What did you do all day?' Flecker inquired.

'Oh, I gave the young horse a school in the paddock and then I caught up with some chores, letter-writing and so on. I was quite glad of a day off I can tell you.' She gave her small, hard laugh. 'I don't get many in the summer I can assure you.'

'Your girl groom wasn't on duty?'

'No, it was Rosemary's Sunday off and since we

weren't going to Upshott I told her she could get off on Saturday as soon as she'd fed and mucked out. That's right, isn't it, Rosemary?'

'Yes, and I caught the nine o'clock bus,' agreed the red-haired girl groom. 'Shall I take him in now, Miss Scott? He's had his fifteen minutes.'

'Yes, take him in and put on another lot of Ref. Lotion,' directed Christina.

Flecker said, 'I know I'm being tiresomely persistent, but we've had a report that you were seen at the show on Saturday afternoon.'

'Who says they saw me there?' demanded Christina.

'That doesn't really matter, does it?' said Flecker.

'Of course it matters if it's their word against mine.'

'You were said to be wearing a navy blue dress and dark glasses,' Flecker told her.

'What nonsense. I haven't a navy blue dress, anyway. I don't like navy, I've never had a navy dress in my life.'

'Well, that sounds conclusive,' said Flecker, putting his envelopes away.

'I suppose one of those secretaries made it up,' said Christina, suddenly filling with righteous indignation. 'Really, how low can people sink? What can they get out of all this vicious tittle-tattle?' She answered herself. 'I suppose their lives are so dull they need a little malicious gossip to brighten them up.'

'I wouldn't have called life with Miss Thistleton dull,' observed Flecker. 'From what I've heard it sounded a hair-raising experience; something like living on the slopes of an active volcano.'

The secretaries had fallen out over their mid-morning coffee. Joy, who was making the most of her holiday, had jeered at the more conscientious Molly, who was religiously devoting all her normal working hours to the sorting, labelling and re-filing of T.T.'s papers.

'I can't think why you want to wear yourself out over that,' Joy had said. 'No one's told you to do it.'

'I can't take Mr. Keswick's money, I mean it wouldn't be right, not to take it and do nothing in return,' Molly had answered.

'It isn't Laurence's money; not yet anyway. We're being paid by the estate and they've got to pay someone to keep the house aired.'

'I don't like to take money from *anyone* without doing something in return, I mean it seems very wrong to *me*,' answered Molly obstinately.

'Well, so long as you don't think you're doing anything productive,' Joy had spoken maliciously, 'because from what I know of your filing and labelling someone will have to do it all over again.'

Molly had protested incoherently against the unkindness and injustice of this remark and when Joy had refused to retract it, she had retired into a hurt silence. They were still in the morning-room rather obviously not speaking when the detectives were shown in by one of the daily women.

Flecker said, 'Good morning, we've come to bother you again, I'm afraid.'

'Oh, it's no *bother*, Chief Inspector, I mean we want to help,' Molly answered as she hurriedly filed a sheaf of letters under the wrong headings.

'We enjoy visitors,' Joy told him, 'at least I do; Molly may regard them as time-wasters interrupting her valuable work.'

'Oh Joy, how can you be so unkind?' exclaimed Molly hotly, and becoming flustered she upset a carton of paper clips, which cascaded in a silver shower all over the carpet. 'Oh dear, I am so clumsy,' she exclaimed piteously. Browning went to her aid and Flecker sat down opposite Joy. 'Two rather frivolous questions first,' he said, looking at his envelopes. 'Why does Mrs. Maggs keep her radio wrapped in newspaper? And have you ever seen Miss Scott wearing navy blue?'

'They do sound a bit off the point,' Joy agreed, 'but I expect there are wheels within wheels. Mrs. Maggs, poor dear, is more than a little dotty. She keeps her wireless wrapped up so that "they" shan't see her. The entire staff tried to persuade her that "they" couldn't see her, but she wouldn't be convinced and when she's tired of an argument she just takes refuge in her deafness.'

'I see,' said Flecker. 'I just wondered. Now what about Miss Scott and navy blue?'

'We don't see much of her out of riding clothes,' answered Joy thoughtfully. 'Of course she's no idea of dressing. She tries to be very feminine and it doesn't suit her; she goes in for frills and bows and floral patterns and she wears décolleté dresses for the evening when she has the shoulders of an ox. I don't remember her in anything as plain and suitable as navy.'

Molly, who was listening to the conversation now that her paper clips were restored to the desk, broke in: 'That wedding, Joy. You know the one I mean. The two show-jumping riders. T.T. only gave them a set of tray cloths and we thought it a bit mingy of her, and then afterwards she was rather cross that she'd gone at all because—' Molly flushed. 'Well, because—'

'Because the infant arrived very shortly afterwards,' Joy interrupted. 'Yes, but what's that got to do with this?'

'Christina was there, don't you remember? Looking much smarter than she usually does, we remarked on it afterwards. She was wearing a two-piece, don't you remember, a navy linen two-piece, saddle-stitched in white.'

'Yes, so she was, but that was two years ago and I've never seen her in it since.'

'Never mind, it's still very interesting,' said Flecker, making a note. Then he looked at his watch. 'Would it disturb you if I came back after lunch and had a session with the scrapbooks?' he asked.

'It won't disturb me,' Joy laughed. 'I'm planning a restful afternoon—a deck chair in the shade. But Molly's engaged on a tremendous reorganization of the filing system; she's trying to impress the executors with her efficiency; I don't know whether she can spare you the room.'

'I wish you wouldn't make fun of me, Joy.' Molly Steer sounded cross as well as hurt. 'Of course the Chief Inspector can have this room. I can easily work somewhere else.'

'But I don't have to look at the scrapbooks *in situ*,' Flecker told her. 'I can have a deck chair in the shade too.'

'No, no,' Molly objected vehemently. 'Of course you

must have the room, it won't inconvenience me at all. I wouldn't dream of not letting you have it, I should be so hurt, I mean—'

'Right you are,' said Flecker hastily as he got to his feet. 'I'll reappear about two. Sandwiches at the Station Hotel and then we'll put you on the train for London,' he said to Browning as they stood for a moment outside the house blinking in the hot, bright sunshine. 'I want you to visit the British Show Jumping Association,' he continued when they were in the car, 'they hang out in Bedford Square. Collect a list of the rules and find out every possible way of cheating that exists.'

Flecker spent the afternoon happily absorbed in the pictorial records of T.T.'s one-sided life. Molly Steer, making frantic efforts not to disturb him, crept in and out at intervals to collect some forgotten paper from filing cabinet or desk; quite unaware that her elephantine creepings were far more disturbing than any normal walk. Her over-zealous efforts for quietude invariably ended by her blundering into a piece of furniture, dropping the stapler or closing the drawers of the metal cabinet with a crash, whereupon she would look anxiously round at Flecker. After the first time, when a stream of abject apologies was invoked by his asking if she had hurt herself, he kept his eyes on the scrapbooks and pretended to be completely engrossed.

When he had finished Flecker wandered out to the garden and found the secretaries drinking tea on the lawn. They pressed him to join them and when the great fuss which arose over a cup and a chair had died down Joy asked whether his search through the scrapbooks had been a success, whether he had found what he wanted.

'I don't altogether know what I want,' Flecker confessed. 'But if one chases all the red herrings with equal assiduity eventually everything is made plain; at least that's my experience.'

'We've had Mrs. Chesterfield on the telephone twice this afternoon trying to catch Mr. Keswick,' Molly told Flecker. 'It's funny, I mean it's peculiar really, that the Down End Farm telephone is disconnected or something, but I suppose they may have forgotten to pay the bill. Anyway, Mr. Keswick hasn't been over and Brenda doesn't expect him until tomorrow morning.'

'Did Mrs. Chesterfield say why she wanted him?' asked Flecker, who thought that he knew.

'No, just that if we saw him to tell him to ring her at once.'

Flecker finished his tea and produced his envelopes. 'There's one point that still puzzles me,' he said. 'So very few people have admitted to knowing of the emergency basket and even fewer to the knowledge of the thermos. Mr. Keswick, for example, knew of the emergency basket, but apparently had no idea that Miss Thistleton drank milk shake. Mrs. Farrell didn't know anything about the emergency basket or thermos. Could Miss Scott have known about them as they were normally carried in the car and not in the horse-box? Did other owners like the Pratts and the Chesterfields see T.T. drinking her milk shake?'

'Helen Farrell knew about the emergency basket,' Joy told him. 'Remember that time at Badminton, Molly, when she broke the shoulder strap of her slip? T.T. sent you all the way to the car park for the emergency basket. Then when you got back after a three-mile walk, Helen didn't want a safety pin. She had taken the slip off in a ditch, using two young cavalry officers as a screen.' Joy laughed. 'Poor old Molly; you should have seen her face,' she told Flecker, 'when she found she'd made the journey for nothing.'

'So Mrs. Farrell knew of the basket,' said Flecker thoughtfully. 'What about the thermos? Could she have seen T.T. taking thirst-quenching draughts?'

'No, I don't think so.' It was Molly who answered. 'You see, I mean T.T. didn't very often drink it; I mean not as often as we took it with us. I mean, as often as not we brought the milk shake home again with us in the evenings. It was like all the other things we took with us; she didn't really need them, but there was terrible unpleasantness if any of them were left behind.'

Flecker looked at her sharply. 'Are you sure about that?' he asked. 'Mrs. Maggs seemed to think that it was very rare for the thermos to come back full.'

The secretaries looked at each other and then Joy gave her whimsical laugh. 'I'd better come clean,' she said. 'I used very often to drink the shake when we got back. You see I'm as anxious to put on weight as Molly is to lose it; and it stopped poor old Maggs feeling that her work was wasted.'

Flecker pushed back his hair and gave a small groan. 'Who knew that you were in the habit of drinking it?' he asked.

'Just Molly, oh and Charity Chesterfield; I told her once when she was going on at me about my being so thin.'

'No one else? Not Miss Dix or either of the Keswicks?'

'No, I don't think so; I don't really see how they could.'

'Who drank it on Friday?'

'No one,' answered Joy. T.T. never asked for it and I didn't get a chance—she was in such a mood when we got home she kept us on the run for hours. Poor old Maggs must have tipped it down the sink.'

Flecker got up. 'Well, thank you,' he said absent-mindedly, 'and thank you for the tea. I must be off.'

He drove back to Hamberley reflecting rather drearily on human nature, on the 'still, sad music of humanity' and on the heredity, the complex fusion of genes, which made one what one was. Freed of Browning's presence he didn't have to disguise his interest in his pigeon-hole at the George, but there was no letter. Lesley hadn't written. He reminded himself that she had no reason to write, that the arrangements for her trip to town were all made, but his heavy and obscure feeling of gloom refused to lighten. It was too early for a drink, so he retired to his bedroom and there, two hours later, Browning found him, coatless and dishevelled, deep in thought and surrounded by a confusion of used envelopes covered in obscure notes.

'Well, they were very helpful,' Browning reported breezily. 'A nice lot of people and there aren't so many ways of cheating after all, not when you get down to it. Do you want to hear about it right away or shall we have dinner?'

'If it's time for dinner we'd better have it,' answered

Flecker, and knowing Browning's dislike of going in late and finding all the best dishes off, he hastily put on his coat.

Browning looked at him disapprovingly. 'You can't go down like that, sir,' he said. 'Your tie's under your left ear and as for your hair—'

'Oh hell,' swore Flecker, making for the mirror.

The small, persistent noises which for some time had been insinuating themselves into Joy's dream suddenly brought her with a jolt to full consciousness. It's only a cat, she told herself, as her meagre body in the faded pink nightdress clung desperately to the soporific well-being of bed. But it didn't sound like a cat, it sounded horribly as though someone was trying to break in. Nonsense, she thought, you're imagining things. You'll end up as silly as Molly. But the small noises persisted. Her heart was hammering with a violence quite out of proportion to her mental fear as she slid out of bed, slipped on her dressing gown and crept to the window. Her bedroom looked, as almost all bedrooms did, over the lawn.

The garden seemed very quiet and still, and strangely shadowed in the silver light. There was no sign of an intruder, but again came the ominous noise. It came from below and from the right. Someone was trying to open the drawing-room french windows. She drew back into the comforting darkness of the room and thought.

She might look a fool if she telephoned the police and it turned out to be a cat, but she wasn't going to risk a closer look. She was still debating whether to put her head under the bedclothes and forget it—after all everything was insured—or to risk a snub and telephone the police, when a crash from downstairs made up her mind for her. 'Help, Joy, help. Burglars, help, police!' squealed Molly's voice from the hall. Joy darted into T.T.'s bedroom, dialled 999 and explained the situation calmly and competently, unmoved by Molly's continued shrieks. As she replaced the receiver she heard a car engine. The police already? she wondered, but decided that it was too soon. There was no sound in the house now. Joy armed herself with one of T.T.'s stout hunting crops and crept out on to the landing. She stood listening intently. Nothing. She began to feel afraid.

Surely nothing could have happened to that fool Molly? But it would be just like her to blunder to a bloody and unnecessary death. She decided to put on the lights. Anything was better than the eerie uncertainty of darkness. She found the switches and simultaneously illuminated the landing, the stairs and the hall.

There was no one to be seen. Cautiously she began to descend the stairs. Halfway down she paused, for though the hall was brightly lit and obviously empty the passage to the kitchen disappeared in a brooding darkness.

Anyone might be lurking there; and the light switch was in the passage itself. Joy turned. It would be safer to await the arrival of the police in a locked bathroom. She began to retreat upstairs, looking anxiously over her shoulder for a pursuer. Then she heard Molly's voice in the morning-room. 'I want the police,' she cried breathlessly; 'tell them to come quickly. Oh, Whittam House—'

'I've already sent for them,' called Joy, exasperation in her voice as her fears departed abruptly. She hurried down to the morning-room. 'You are a fool, Molly, I rang them hours ago. They're on their way.'

Molly, trembling with fright, trying to answer Joy and to explain to the police that they had already been summoned, became quite incoherent and Joy snatched the receiver from her and explained what had happened herself. They were still wrangling contentiously over who was to blame for the muddle when the local patrol car came racing down the drive and stopped with a dramatic scrunch of tyres on gravel. Molly, suddenly becoming aware that her only garment was a low-cut and almost transparent nightdress, fled upstairs as Joy hurried to open the front door.

'You're too late, I think he's gone,' she told the sergeant who precipitated himself into the hall. 'It sounded as though he was trying to break into the drawing-room, there,' she indicated the door and watched from a discreet distance as the sergeant burst in. But the room was empty and the windows still closed. 'He didn't get in then,' said the sergeant, opening a french window and stepping out on the lawn where two constables appeared from the shadows to join him.

'I'll go and dress,' Joy called to them.

While the secretaries dressed another police car arrived carrying, among other things, photographic equipment, and, shortly afterwards, Flecker and Browning drove up, having been summoned by the Hamberley police when they realised that it was the murdered woman's house that was involved. The detectives, unshaven and still slightly bemused by their sudden awakening, joined the group round the drawing-room windows, on one pair of which an amateur-looking attempt at breaking in had been found.

'Looks as though he tried to lever them open with a screwdriver, sir,' the uniformed sergeant told Flecker, 'but he knew enough to wear gloves.'

Having arranged for one party to search the house and the other the grounds, Flecker interviewed the secretaries.

'You don't think it was just the imagination of a couple of hysterical women?' asked Joy.

Flecker shook his head. 'No, someone did try to get in.'

'Oh, do you think it was the murderer coming back?' Molly, her pale eyes goggling behind the green spectacles, sounded terrified. 'I mean he might have come back to find some evidence or something. Or do you think Joy and I know something and he meant—he meant to murder us?' She gazed intently at Flecker, almost beseeching reassurance.

'I don't know yet,' Flecker told her, 'but I'll leave you a police guard until we've sorted it out.'

'Oh, Joy, supposing he had got in? We might have been murdered,' Molly wailed.

'Don't make such a fuss, Molly. He didn't get in and he didn't murder us, so there's nothing to wail about,' Joy told her sharply.

'It's all very well for you to be so brave about it, but I was much nearer him than you were, I came downstairs.'

'I came downstairs as soon as any useful purpose could be served by it.' Joy spoke with asperity. 'I had the sense to telephone the police from *upstairs* first. And, if you hadn't started shrieking he wouldn't have been frightened off and the police would have caught him red-handed,' she added triumphantly.

'How can you be so unkind?' protested Molly. 'I ran into the umbrella stand in the dark and having made all that noise what could I do but call for help?'

'Did either of you see anything of the would-be intruder?' asked Flecker, growing tired of their wrangling.

'No,' Joy answered at once. 'I looked for him out of my bedroom window, but the first floor of the house overhangs a bit and you can't see the french windows.'

'And when you were telephoning,' asked Flecker, 'did you hear anyone making off? Footsteps on the gravel or anything?'

'No footsteps, but I heard a car start.'

'A car. Did it sound as though it was close? I mean, just outside the house?' asked Flecker.

'I'm no expert', Joy answered. 'It's donkeys' years since I've driven, but it certainly wasn't just outside the house. It was quite loud though. It must have been about half-way up the drive I should think.'

Flecker turned to Browning. 'Would you take a look?' he said. And as Browning left the room, he went on, 'Now, Miss Steer, your turn. What did you see and hear?'

Flecker was still disentangling Molly's long, confused story when Browning reappeared with a triumphant expression on his face and a sheet of paper in his hand. He laid the paper before Flecker. On it he had written, 'Looks as though he left it in shrubbery, right-hand side, top of drive. Land Rover with a fairly worn set of heavy duty tyres and a slight oil leak in either the back axle or the differential box.'

'Good,' said Flecker getting to his feet. 'One last question, Miss Hemming. Have you told anyone else what you told me about your drinking the milk shake?'

'Only Charity Chesterfield,' Joy answered. 'She telephoned again to ask whether Laurence had turned up and then she went on to talk about the murder and I told her about the milk shake.'

'And you, Miss Steer?'

'I haven't told anyone, not a soul,' Molly answered him.

CHAPTER SEVEN

IT WAS JUST after nine on Saturday morning when Flecker and Browning, after only a few hours' sleep, reappeared at Whittam House. Having checked with the constable on duty that there'd been no further disturbances, the detectives drove round to the stables. One Land Rover, coupled to its trailer, waited on the gravel sweep.

'Our first customer,' said Browning, parking the police car beside it. He got out and gave the Land Rover's tyres a casual glance. 'Not guilty,' he told Flecker. 'Too new a job altogether.'

In the stable they found Helen Farrell grooming her horse and Brenda Dix mucking out.

'Good morning; no Mr. Keswick?' inquired Flecker.

Helen looked up. The hideous green-blue bruise and the half-closed eye seemed almost sacrilege on that lovely face. 'Laurence isn't coming to the show,' she said shortly.

'Why not?' asked Flecker.

'God knows. Both his horses are entered and five of T.T.'s. He's chucking away pounds in entry fees.' She body-brushed her horse in short, angry strokes.

'Is he still up at Down End?' asked Flecker.

'He was last night. He's had the telephone disconnected —he says he wants some peace. If you ask me he's off his rocker.'

'We're going to shatter the peace,' said Flecker grinning. 'Any messages?'

But Helen had lost interest in him.

'Be a saint and fill my hay net,' she called down the stable to the already overworked Brenda, 'I'm never going to get there at this rate.'

The yard at Down End Farm appeared to be empty and Browning, observing Keswick's Land Rover standing in an open-fronted implement shed, suggested, 'A quick dekko, we can always make out I was looking for him.'

'Right you are. The less they know about our interests the better, considering how they telephone each other. I'll go on towards the house.'

A few moments later Browning overtook Flecker. 'No, it's not him,' he said, shaking his head. 'No oil leak and two new tyres. What's Miss Scott got besides that sports car?'

'A horse-box, I suspect,' answered Flecker. 'She had some very outsize doors on her garage.'

'And Mrs. Pratt's only got that old rattle-trap,' observed Browning sadly as Flecker knocked on the door. There was a truculent sound about Keswick's footsteps as he came down the passage. He flung open the door and looked as though he were about to loose an angry stream of words, but his expression changed when he saw the detectives.

'Oh, it's you,' he said, as though pleasantly surprised. 'Come in. I've just made some coffee, would you like some?'

They followed him into the kitchen, which was in a state of considerable confusion, and Keswick advanced on the cluttered sink. 'I wash them when I want them,' he announced rather defiantly. 'I can't see that it matters whether one washes up before or after meals—the total time and energy expended it exactly the same. Tea spoons, tea spoons,' he muttered, searching among the miscellaneous objects which covered the draining board.

They took their cups of coffee into the sitting-room, which had grown several degrees dustier since the detectives' last visit. When they had disposed themselves about the room Flecker said, 'I gather you're not going to the show today.'

'You gather correctly,' answered Keswick, in a voice which forbade further questioning on that subject.

'I also gather that you have severed communication with the outside world. Mrs. Chesterfield is very anxious to get in touch with you.'

'Yes, I told the telephone people not to put through any more calls. The Sunday papers wanted my memoirs "as told to our reporter," Mrs. Farrell seemed to require endless sympathy for that black eye and Christina Scott wants to ride T.T.'s horses for me. She's been throwing out rather obvious hints for several days, but when she heard I wasn't going to ride them at Hallam myself she rang up with all sorts of propositions for sharing the lolly. Though why she suddenly expects to start winning again, I can't imagine. Anyway she wouldn't take no for an answer and she began to hint that I ought to rise above my dog-in-the-manger nature. I'm afraid I lost my temper. Do you know what Charity wanted?'

Flecker shook his head.

'I'd telephone her, but she'll be at Hallam all day.'

'We're going along too,' Browning told him.

'In the character of detectives?' asked Keswick. 'But what on earth for? I mean what do you hope to discover there?'

'Background, background,' Flecker answered with a grin, 'and we've a few details to look into.' He pulled his envelopes out of his pocket and began to sort through them in a leisurely manner. Then he looked up at Keswick. 'I know you've already said that you didn't go near Miss Thistleton's horse-box last Saturday, but that was in the context of near enough to put poison in the milk shake. I wonder if during the day you weren't *somewhere* near; near enough to have been seen coming away from the direction of the box?'

Keswick scratched his head thoughtfully and then became slightly embarrassed. 'Yes,' he answered. 'I think that could have happened. I had a bit of luck. I won the Upshott Shield and fifty pounds; I was feeling rather flush and it occurred to me that perhaps my wife could do with a contribution towards the housekeeping. I went over towards T.T.'s box, but Marion didn't seem to be about so I gave up the idea.'

'I see. And do you remember Mr. Frogmorton telling you about the lethal potentialities of linseed?' asked Flecker.

'Linseed?' repeated Keswick, looking puzzled. 'Oh yes, of course, the Pratt pony. Oh, I see what you're getting at.' He looked hard at Flecker. 'That was prussic acid too.'

'Yes.'

'Does this mean that you suspect me of murdering my cousin?' he asked, a note of belligerence in his voice.

'Not particularly,' Flecker answered equably. 'Mr. Frogmorton assures me that he and his assistants have told all the horse owners in the district that prussic acid can be released from linseed. No doubt most of them were at the Upshott Show.'

'But I'm the one who inherits a quarter of a million, less estate duties,' suggested Keswick.

'True,' agreed Flecker getting to his feet, 'but still, money isn't the only motive for murder.'

Keswick looked amused. 'Well, in exchange for those few kind words I'll provide you with a ringside car park ticket and a couple of members' guest badges,' he said. He chose one from a selection of envelopes propped along the mantelpiece and sorted through the contents. 'There you are, they're not mine,' he added, as the detectives began to thank him. 'I've never been able to do things in style. They're T.T.'s, but it seems very fitting that her avengers should go as her guests.'

'We *are* coming up in the world', said Browning, as he settled himself in the car. He attached his enclosure badge to his buttonhole and squinted down at it complacently.

'Very nice too,' he observed, 'but as things have turned out,' he added, looking critically at Flecker, 'it's a pity you didn't put on your better suit.'

'Oh hell, we're not going to the Royal Enclosure at Ascot,' Flecker told him, 'and anyway it's going to rain.'

'And you with no mackintosh. We'd better turn back, hadn't we, and fetch it from Frailford?'

'No', Flecker answered firmly. 'It won't kill me to get wet. Come on, step on it or you'll miss the jumping.'

'Every Land Rover in the country', said Browning cheerfully as he drove past the car park and on towards the ring.

'I've a shrewd suspicion,' remarked Flecker, 'that we shall only need to look at one.'

In the ring a competitor was jumping. 'Nothing very big there,' observed Browning, looking at the course. 'I expect it's just the Grade C.'

As Flecker climbed out of the car the first rain fell; a few isolated drops that were ominously large. 'I don't suppose it's any use looking for competitors in the enclosure,' said Flecker, gazing dubiously at the busy scene. 'We'd better try the collecting ring, if we can find it.'

Helen Farrell was sitting on her shooting stick by the collecting-ring entrance, her lovely face further marred by an expression of discontent. 'Good morning again,' said Flecker, 'have you performed yet?'

'No, the absolute imbeciles have mucked the whole thing up. They had so many entries they've divided the Grade C into two sections and they sent the postcard telling me that I'm in the second section, to London, so of course I haven't had it. I'm not in till three. I could kill them. All that rushing about to get here and now I've got to wait *hours*.'

'Isn't there time to go home and come back again?' suggested Flecker.

'It's such a stinking waste of petrol, besides all the bother of loading and unloading the horse,' she pointed out angrily.

It began to rain harder as the detectives wandered

through the horse-box park, looking for the Chesterfield Land Rover. It was Browning who observed Marion Keswick hastily gathering an armful of horse equipment that was strewn around a trailer, and bundling it in the back of a Land Rover.

'There we are,' he said, and, 'Better run for it, hadn't we?' They turned up their coat collars and ran through the downpour. Marion was fumbling with the back flap of the Land Rover, trying to close it against the rain; Flecker went to help her while Browning walked round, glancing casually at the tyres of the Land Rover and then peered underneath. He nodded grimly as he rejoined Flecker. Flecker turned to Marion. 'Is Mrs. Chesterfield about?' he asked.

'She's on the showground,' Marion answered, 'but she went off with Sarah to find a place for a practice jump. There's no room even to exercise up this end.'

'Will you shelter us,' asked Flecker, 'until she turns up?'

'Yes, all right.' Marion looked at them apprehensively. 'There's room for three in front and you can watch what's going on in the ring; there's a sort of natural grandstand here; the ground rises, Charity remembered from last year.' She climbed into the driver's seat and started the windscreen wipers. 'Charity doesn't seem to bother about the battery,' she told them as they crowded in beside her.

'Not much of a performance,' observed Browning disapprovingly as a competitor refused three times at the first fence and left the ring.

'I expects it's the rain,' said Marion; 'it upsets most

horses.'

Flecker produced a collection of damp envelopes from his pocket and began to study them in a preoccupied manner. A wild and untrained grey horse, carrying his head horizontally, proceeded round the ring at the gallop, demolishing every fence in its path. 'Not a very high standard,' said Browning in dissatisfied tones.

Flecker turned to Marion. 'Did you have any disturbances last night?' he asked.

'Disturbances?' Marion repeated doubtfully. 'I don't think so.'

'Someone tried to break into Whittam House,' Flecker told her, 'but the secretaries frightened whoever it was off.'

'Well, we certainly didn't have any burglars,' answered Marion and then, catching sight of a sturdy figure completely enveloped in a very long mackintosh and a large yellow sou'-wester, she added with relief, 'Oh, here *is* Charity.'

Charity Chesterfield looked vaguely at the detectives as they climbed out of the Land Rover and announced, 'That obstinate fool of a collecting steward, he's making the children jump according to their numbers and the whole show is going to be held up for hours while the ones with several ponies change from one to the next. Sarah's going twenty-eighth and she's soaked to the skin already.'

Marion said, 'Oh dear,' and, 'Chief Inspector Flecker wants to ask you something.'

But Charity was looking at the ring where the stewards were altering the fences for the next class.

'Go on,' she said, 'put them down. Lower than that. You can't expect the poor kids to jump much in this.'

Flecker asked, 'Where do you keep the key of your Land Rover, Mrs. Chesterfield?'

'The key of the Land Rover,' said Charity, looking at him with unfocused eyes. 'Oh, anywhere. In the Land Rover generally, or in my pocket.'

'What about at night?' asked Flecker.

'Oh, sometimes I put it on the hall table. Look, there's the Graham child, stopped again, I can't think why they bother with that pony.'

'What about *last* night?' asked Flecker.

Charity looked at him vaguely. 'Oh, the key. Probably I left it on the hall table. Here's a Pratt, the little one; I expect she'll go clear.'

'Last night then you, Mrs. Keswick, or presumably your son could have taken the Land Rover out without the others being aware of it,' said Flecker, showing less patience than usual as the rain trickled down his neck.

Marion said, 'Charity, do attend. Someone tried to break into Whittam House last night.' She looked at Flecker. 'But I don't see what this Land Rover's got to do with it.'

Charity pulled herself together abruptly. 'Hugh can't go out alone,' she said, 'he failed his test.'

Flecker pushed back a lock of wet hair and said, 'Did any of you take the Land Rover to Whittam at any time yesterday?'

'No, we didn't go near the place,' Charity answered firmly. Flecker looked at Marion.

'No, I've only driven it once and that was down to the

village when we ran out of salt.'

'Right,' said Flecker. 'Well, last night someone attempted to break into Whittam House. We think whoever it was came in a Land Rover with an oil leak and a set of fairly worn tyres. Your Land Rover,' he looked at Charity, 'has an oil leak and a fairly worn set of tyres and so, naturally, I'm inquiring into its whereabouts last night. Is your son here?'

Charity's ruddy face had taken on a greyish tinge, but her voice was unshaken. 'No, he isn't,' she answered, 'and there must be thousands of Land Rovers with oil leaks.'

'Yes, I expect there are,' admitted Flecker equably. 'Is Hugh at home?'

'No, he's gone out for the day with a friend. I don't expect him back much before supper.'

'I'll come round this evening then,' said Flecker.

As the detectives hurried through the drizzling rain to sample the delights of the members' enclosure Marion and Charity sat damply in the Land Rover, both wearing worried expressions.

'Why should it be your Land Rover?' asked Marion; 'and why should Hugh have gone to Whittam House in the middle of the night? The police have gone mad.'

'Yes, that's it, the police have gone mad,' repeated Charity in unconvinced tones. She looked away from Marion. 'Hugh's been behaving so very oddly lately,' she said in a strained voice.

Marion, finding the position reversed and herself in the role of comforter, hastily prised her mind from its preoccupation with her own affairs.

'But what *could* Hugh have to do with it?' she asked earnestly. 'Apart from being Hugh, there's no reason why he should be mixed up in T.T.'s murder; after all she was about to change her will in favour of Hugh and Sarah.'

'Yes, I suppose you're right,' agreed Charity, but all her usual ebullience had left her. She sagged in her seat, looking old and grey and beaten. 'I don't know, I can't tell what he feels; I don't know him any more, Marion. It's like being confronted with a stranger, a suspicious, unfriendly stranger. And he used to be such a dear little boy—'

'But isn't it a stage all adolescents go through?' asked Marion.

Charity made a valiant effort at self-control. She turned her gaze back to the ring. 'Look,' she said in a trembling voice, 'one of the Farquharson twins on the pony they bought from the Pratts. Have you ever seen so many martingales and nosebands?' But she couldn't recapture her interest in the show; she even watched Sarah's round in dismal silence and when the gate fell, giving her four faults and putting her out of the competition, Charity felt almost glad. Now they could go home, get warm and dry and ready to talk to Hugh.

Marion, damp and miserable, feeling extraordinarily flat, having bolstered herself up for a glimpse of Laurence that had not materialized, and filled with a vague alarm by Charity's manner, was also pleased to leave the show. Willingly she collected the crestfallen Sarah's possessions and helped to rub down and box the dripping pony.

'They'll need tractors to pull those horse-boxes out,' observed Charity gloomily as she drove slowly from the ground.

In the ring, the two younger Pratts were jumping off against each other for first place. With grim efficiency they cleared the enormous fences, both, apparently, quite unmoved by the weather, the slippery ground and the wet reins which slithered through their ungloved hands. They were watched only by their mother, two very irritable judges and a few spectators who, having paid for their ringside car park, were unwilling to go home. Browning, whose opinion of the Pratts was now tempered with a reluctant respect, followed the competition closely, but though Flecker looked in the direction of the ring his thoughts were elsewhere; he was gloomily regretting that the maintenance of law and order should always leave such a trail of shattered lives in its wake.

Laurence Keswick had divided the day between exercising his horses and tending his pigs and poultry and bitter reflection on the situation in which he found himself. At five o'clock he drove towards Frailford, judging that by then Charity would be home from the show. He suspected, from her constant attempts to reach him on the telephone, that she was acting as an emissary from his wife and as he drove he determined that he would end what he had begun to describe to himself as 'all this nonsense' one way or the other. But, let into the farmhouse by a tearful-looking Sarah, he found himself in the middle of a family scene. Charity, who'd quite abandoned her usual calm common sense, was shrieking at Hugh in desperate and despairing fury. Hugh, his fair hair hanging over his thin white face, his eyes avoiding his mother's, had the hunted look of a cornered animal. 'Why don't you leave me alone? It's nothing to do with you, is it?' he was shouting as Laurence, gently restraining the enthusiastic welcome of the bull terrier, came to the doorway of the sitting-room.

Marion, huddled in a low chair close to the electric fire, said, 'Oh Hugh, she's only trying to help; we'll all help if only—' she stopped as she saw her husband. Charity said, 'Laurence, thank God. Perhaps you can make him see sense.'

With a certain relief, Keswick shelved his own problems. 'What's he been up to?' he asked.

'That's what he won't tell us. He won't say if it was him at Whittam last night and the police are coming. We've got to decide what to say. Hugh, can't you see that we must all tell them the same story?' Charity sounded frantic with fear and Keswick looked mystified. 'You don't mean you're accusing Hugh of attempted burglary last night?' he asked.

'The detectives think whoever it was went there in Charity's Land Rover,' Marion explained. 'It's leaking oil or something.'

'But why on earth should Hugh—?' asked Keswick.

'All right then, it was me,' Hugh shouted suddenly. 'There, now you know and a lot of good it'll do you. And I don't want your bloody help either. Let the police come, I don't care—'

'Hugh, don't be childish.' Keswick tried to sound calm

and capable, though he felt himself being carried away by Charity's obvious terror and the general uproar. But Hugh suddenly rushed from the room. They heard his feet thundering upstairs and then a door slammed and a key turned in a lock. Charity ran halfway up the stairs. 'Oh God, he's locked himself in the bathroom. There's a razor in there. Oh God, now what's he going to do?' she cried. She ran on up the stairs and began to beat on the bathroom door. 'Hugh, come out of there. What are you doing? Come out of there at once,' she sobbed, the last vestige of her self-control departing.

The Keswicks looked at each other appalled.

'Can he really be mixed up in this?' asked Laurence.

'I don't know.' Marion drew a hand across her eyes. 'She's so frightened there must be something we don't know about.'

'Well, the obvious thing is to get hold of a good solicitor,' said Keswick, hurrying upstairs. As Marion turned to comfort Sarah there was a knock on the front door. The police, she thought, and began to wonder whether delaying tactics would be any use. But there was no point in prolonging the agony, she decided, and if Hugh was really committing suicide they might be some use. She hastily opened the door. Flecker looked at her worried face and listened for a moment to the commotion upstairs. Then he asked, 'Hugh?' Marion said, 'Yes, we don't know what's the matter, but he's locked himself in the bathroom.'

Flecker ran upstairs, followed by Browning, Marion and Sarah.

'All right, Mrs. Chesterfield,' he said. 'We'll get him

out.'

'There's not a sound,' moaned Charity. 'What's he doing in there?'

'Have you a ladder?' Flecker asked.

'Yes, it's behind the garage,' Sarah answered at once.

'Right, well you show my sergeant and Mr. Keswick where to find it. Mrs. Keswick, take Mrs. Chesterfield downstairs and make her a cup of tea. I want a quiet word with Hugh,' he added, when they all showed a disinclination to move.

'Come along, madam,' said Browning, taking the distraught Charity by the arm. 'You leave it to the Chief Inspector.'

'Why doesn't he break the door down?' moaned Charity as she was led away.

Flecker waited until they were all downstairs and then he knocked gently on the bathroom door. 'Hugh,' he said, 'it's Chief Inspector Flecker here. I want that scrapbook. Don't you think you'd better come out and give it to me?' There was no response. He waited a little and then tried again. 'You can't spend the rest of your life in there,' he pointed out. 'Come on, save me the trouble of climbing in at the window or breaking down the door.'

He was just beginning to wonder whether the boy had done something silly when the key turned in the lock, the door opened slowly and Hugh appeared, his white face blotched with tears. He looked at Flecker. 'You'd better arrest me,' he said, 'I'm a thief.'

'Well yes, I had rather guessed that,' answered Flecker calmly. 'Come on, we'll go downstairs and talk it over quietly.'

In the hall they met Browning and Keswick who, having placed the ladder in position, had appeared for further orders.

'Oh good, you've got him out,' said Keswick. 'I don't think you ought to question him except in the presence of his mother and a solicitor.' Charity rushed out of the kitchen. 'Don't say anything,' she cried. 'Hugh, you're not to say a word. Where's the telephone directory? Oh Marion, find Geoffrey Haines's number.'

Flecker said, 'All these precautions are quite unnecessary.' He pushed back his hair in an exasperated gesture. 'Look, I haven't charged Hugh with anything. I am not at this stage contemplating charging him with anything. He's seventeen and that's quite old enough to talk to a policeman alone.'

'And she's not my mother,' shouted Hugh with a sudden hysterical venom that made Flecker push him hastily into the sitting-room and shut the door. 'Now sit down,' he said, 'and for heaven's sake keep calm.'

Hugh seated himself gingerly on the extreme edge of the sofa, so Flecker chose one of the armchairs. 'What did you want the money for?' he asked.

Hugh's thin body contorted almost as though in physical pain; he stared fixedly at the hearthrug. 'I owed it,' he said in a shaking voice, 'to a bookmaker.'

'How did you manage that?' asked Flecker. 'Bookmakers aren't generally stupid enough to let people of your age have accounts.'

'A boy at school has an elder brother in the army, he puts it on for us,' Hugh explained. 'It all began when we hitch-hiked to the races on a Saturday. Colin's brother was there with some friends. I soon lost all my money. I hadn't much, but Colin's brother lent me a whole lot more. I lost that too. He was very sorry about it and the next week he rang us up at school to say he'd heard of an absolute certainty and we must all recover our losses by backing it. So he put some more money on for me and that horse lost too.'

'Certainties make a habit of it,' said Flecker. 'Go on, what happened next?'

'Colin's brother wanted to be paid back. He was quite decent about it, but he'd lost a lot and his mess-bill came in or something. I sold my camera, but it wasn't a particularly good one and I hadn't anything else that was worth anything.'

'You couldn't tell your adopted mother?' asked Flecker.

Hugh shook his head. 'She hasn't any spare cash. Not with two of us at school. School fees are enormous nowadays,' he answered gloomily.

'So you went to Whittam House last Saturday,' prompted Flecker.

'Yes. I'd had another letter from Colin on Friday asking if I couldn't do something. I decided to ask T.T. to lend me the money. All Friday at the show I kept hoping to speak to her; I waited in the enclosure all day, but I didn't get a chance; the secretaries never seemed to leave her. On Saturday I made up my mind I'd go to Whittam, wait till she got home, and ask to see her alone. There was no one about, and no one answered the door, but I found the french windows open, so I went in and waited in the drawing-room. The scrapbook was there on the table so I looked through it as I waited. I saw the money, it was pasted in in cellophane packets and labelled 1st and 2nd prizes at the South Roscott show or something. It wasn't doing anyone any good. I waited for ages and then at last I heard the car come back and the secretaries in the hall; they were shouting at Mrs. Maggs trying to explain that T.T. was dead. When I heard that I picked up the scrapbook, went out through the window and ran. It seemed the only thing to do.'

'What about last night?' said Flecker.

Hugh buried his face in his hands. 'They kept on and on about the scrapbook,' he explained. 'Marion and my mother, I mean. They seemed to think if it could be found it would solve everything. In the end I decided to take it back. I thought I'd put it somewhere in the drawing-room, somewhere not too obvious so that it could have been there all the time.'

'Why didn't you just leave it on the doorstep?' asked Flecker.

'I didn't want to draw everyone's attention to it,' Hugh answered. 'I went through it several times rubbing off fingerprints, but I couldn't be certain there weren't some left.'

'I see,' said Flecker. 'Now what about your parentage? I take it you are adopted?'

'Yes, you see my parents were old when they married; my mother was nearly forty and my father even older, and when no children arrived they thought they weren't going to have any so they adopted me. Then Sarah arrived.'

'Tiresome,' said Flecker. 'And you felt they preferred Sarah to you?'

'They didn't say so or anything,' Hugh answered. 'It's just that she's always been much more satisfactory. She's mad about horses and good-tempered like my mother and all that sort of thing. The point is that she's like them and I'm not; I'm different.'

Now that the formidable wall of his introversion was breached, the boy was obviously glad to talk about himself, thought Flecker, watching Hugh's eyes light up and become able to meet his own.

'Of course other people don't realise I'm adopted,' Hugh went on. 'They're always saying that I've got my mother's nose or something, you know how people do. But the odd thing is I am a bit like her. I suppose it's having lived with her for so long: you know, like dogs getting like their owners or the other way round.'

'You don't know who your real parents were?' asked Flecker.

'No.' Hugh shook his head. 'They got me through an adoption society. I suppose I was left on a doorstep or something, but none of the societies will tell you anything about the real parents.'

'Which gives the children unlimited opportunity for wild surmise as they grow up?' suggested Flecker.

Hugh blushed. 'Yes, I suppose so. But still, anything might be true.'

'Who did know you were adopted?'

'No one much. Relations and some old friends of my parents. Laurence Keswick's about the only person round here who knows. My mother told him because she altered her will after my father died and made Laurence one of our guardians.'

'Good,' said Flecker getting to his feet. 'Well, we'll explain the situation to him now.'

As Flecker had feared, his request for Keswick to come in brought Charity hurrying from the kitchen to demand instant elucidation.

'Yes, in a minute,' Flecker told her patiently. 'He hasn't done anything too disastrous and we're just getting things sorted out.'

'Come along, madam. You leave it to the Chief Inspector, he's used to dealing with this sort of situation,' said Browning soothingly as he shepherded her away.

Laurence Keswick looked inquiringly from Hugh to Flecker and waited. Flecker retold Hugh's story as briefly as possible. 'Strictly speaking I suppose I ought to charge him with larceny,' he went on, 'but it seems rather unnecessary, he'll only be wasting some overworked probation officer's time. How do you feel about it? As chief beneficiary the scrapbook and its contents are really your property; do you want me to go any further or can you sort it out between you?'

'I certainly don't want you to go any further if it can be avoided,' answered Laurence slowly. 'I mean if you can turn a blind eye without breaking any police regulations I think we'd all be extremely grateful. It sounds to me as though Hugh's got himself into a stupid mess rather than a criminal one.'

'Well, as far as I'm concerned no loss has been reported,' Flecker explained, 'and as it's more or less in the family—anyway, I'll have a word with the Chief

Constable about it. And now,' he went on briskly as he turned to Hugh, 'I'd like that scrapbook; I hope you haven't been ill-treating it?'

'No,' Hugh answered. 'It's O.K. I hid it in the loft, in the trunk with the bee-keeping outfits, all among the straw hats and veils; it may have a faint old-lady smell.' There was a note of hysterical humour in his voice which irritated Laurence. 'I can't think why you didn't tell your mother you were in a mess, instead of causing all this uproar,' he said severely. 'Or why, if you couldn't tell her, you didn't come and borrow from me.' At this reproach Hugh's shame overwhelmed him again. He stood hanging his head in an attitude of gangling abjection.

'I did think of it,' he said, 'but everyone I knew seemed so hard up, except for T.T.'

'Go and get that scrapbook,' Flecker told him, 'and don't hurry over it, because while you're out of the way I'm going to explain things to your mother.'

Flecker sent Keswick to enlighten Marion, Browning and Sarah while he explained matters more fully to the distraught and exhausted Charity. He did his best to lighten her grief and gloom. He pointed out that much wilder oats had often been sown by what were now exemplary citizens. That the unnamed elder brother had been largely to blame, and that Hugh had learned a valuable lesson without much harm being done. But Charity seemed to have gained only a temporary respite from terror. She was, thought Flecker, behaving like someone who has survived the first wave of attack, but is too frightened of what will follow for even a moment's self-congratulation or thanksgiving.

He took her back to the kitchen and they were all standing about drinking tea and searching for subjects of conversation when Hugh, looking shamefaced and avoiding his mother's and sister's eyes, came in with the scrapbook and handed it to Flecker.

'Do you think that it will tell you what you want to know?' asked Marion diffidently. 'Do you think it will solve the crime?'

'I hope it's going to tell me what was in T.T.'s mind on Friday evening,' Flecker answered her. 'That should solve one bit of the puzzle, but not all. I suspect that most of what I need to know is being carefully guarded from me. I think that if everyone in this room suddenly decided to tell me all he or she knew the investigation would be finished and the crime solved without any further effort on my part.'

'What *do* you mean?' demanded Laurence. 'That seems to me an incredible statement to make.'

'Well, time will show,' answered Flecker equably. He drank the rest of his tea and put down his cup. 'We must be on our way.'

'Your mackintosh, sir,' Browning reminded him reproachfully, 'don't let us forget it again.' Flecker, who'd been watching Marion across the table, ignored him. 'Look out,' he called to Keswick, 'your wife's going to faint.' Marion, realizing it herself at the same moment, was swaying as she groped blindly for a chair. Laurence caught her as her legs buckled and sat her down at the table. Confronted with the need for action Charity immediately became competent; she sent Sarah for a glass of water, Hugh to the dining-room for brandy, while she tried to persuade the ashen Marion to put her head between her knees. Browning began to offer extraneous advice.

'Come on,' Flecker said to him, 'we're not usefully employed; we're merely taking up space and consuming valuable oxygen,' and he led the way out. Laurence, an expression of rising rage on his long face, followed them. Closing the kitchen door behind him, he turned on Flecker furiously. 'You caused that,' he said, 'with your idiotic innuendoes. Why can't you leave my wife alone? If you've got a case against her, let's hear it. Let's bring it out into the open and we'll get a solicitor to advise us; otherwise, leave her alone.'

Flecker looked up at him. 'I don't think it was me, you know,' he answered calmly. 'Well, perhaps I was a contributing factor at the end of a long and very tiring day, but the basic reason has nothing to do with me.'

'What are you talking about?' demanded Keswick angrily.

Flecker looked at him for a moment, searched for words and then suddenly grinned. 'Didn't anyone ever tell you,' he asked, 'about the birds and the bees?'

Keswick stood and stared and gradually comprehension wiped the anger from his face.

'Good God, is that it?' he said. 'Is that what's been causing all the trouble?' He turned and hurried back to the kitchen.

'Well, well,' observed Browning as he and Flecker let themselves out. 'It did just enter my mind.'

CHAPTER EIGHT

LAURENCE KESWICK went back into the kitchen and stood gazing down on his wan-faced wife. Marion looked up at him. 'I'm all right now,' she said unconvincingly in tremulous tones.

Charity turned to Hugh and Sarah. 'Do you think you two could put the Land Rover and trailer away?' she asked. 'We were so wet and cold,' she explained to Hugh, 'we just left it in the yard, but it seems to have stopped raining now.'

'Yes, I'll do it.' Hugh sounded eager to be of use. Now that the first terrible shame of discovery was wearing off, he felt curiously empty; limp and washed-out by emotion, but miraculously free. Sarah, longing to escape from the adult world with its complex scenes and unexplained tensions, followed him willingly.

Laurence sat down on the plastic-covered table, looked at his wife again and said, 'The police seem to think you're pregnant.'

Marion flushed pinkly and looked down at the clenched hands in her lap.

'Oh, Marion, why didn't you tell us?' demanded Charity reproachfully. And then with indignation, 'You silly girl, look what you've been doing: dragging jumps about and heaving up that trailer ramp.'

'Are you?' asked Laurence quietly.

Still looking away from him, Marion answered miserably, 'Yes, I think so.'

Laurence got up. 'Well, that just about explains

everything,' he said with forced cheerfulness.

'No, it doesn't. And it's no use dismissing the whole business as the tantrums of a pregnant woman, because it wasn't.' Marion spoke with a weary urgency. 'And anyway, Laurence, it doesn't make any difference.' She sought for words. 'I mean you don't have to come back just because of this.'

'I think it makes all the difference in the world,' Laurence told her. 'We quarrelled originally because you kept nagging at me about security and I thought you were being bloody unreasonable. If we're having a baby, I don't think you're being unreasonable or only moderately so.' He turned to Charity. 'Oughtn't she to go to bed or lie down or something?'

'No,' Marion answered first. 'I'm perfectly all right now; it was all that standing—'

'I'd take her home,' Laurence went on, 'but I know she'll start on the housework or the washing up. Could you cope with her for another couple of days, Charity, until I've cleaned up the place a bit and got some sort of help?'

'Yes, of course.' Charity forced some warmth into her tired voice. 'Now go on, Marion, upstairs with you and lie down until supper. I've got Hugh and Sarah to help me.'

'Yes, come on, be tactful.' Laurence turned on his wife firmly. 'Leave the Chesterfields to themselves for an hour—'

Later on that evening, after clearing the backlog of washing up in a mood of virtuous energy, Laurence Keswick drove down to the George and spent an unpleasant and recriminatory quarter of an hour with Helen Farrell. Afterwards, reviving himself with a drink in the bar on the way out, he learned from Stan that the detectives had returned to London for what was left of the weekend, and were not expected back until Monday evening.

Sunday was fine. A day of blue and gold, but the heat of the sun was tempered and the air soberly autumnal. Browning spent the greater part of the day trimming his already neat privet hedge, an occupation which provided unlimited opportunity for conversation with the neighbours. Flecker took the Sunday papers to Kensington Gardens, but, growing tired of the to-do that was made over the perpetual ebb and flow of world affairs, he abandoned them and, lying on the grass, watched the people. He found himself envying the men with girls; the fathers with children, and began to wish that he had had the presumption—or was it the courage?—to go down and visit Lesley at her parents' house in Hove.

The Chesterfields and Marion went to church, where they prayed passionately but egocentrically for themselves and each other. Laurence Keswick joined them for lunch and they waded through the substantial meal, treating each other with anxious solicitude and concealing behind a facade of polite conversation, emotions which varied from a bowel-gnawing fear, unallayable because it took no definite shape, to a despairing dread of discovery that was no more bearable for being known and faced.

After lunch Hugh and Sarah went off to play tennis and their elders sat in the garden. They sat drinking in the warm air, heavy with the scent of the late roses and listening to the white pigeons which cooed softly from the stable roof and to the occasional long, weary thud as an apple fell in the orchard. And the faint melancholy of fulfilment, the haunting undertones of sadness with which autumn seems to mourn the death of the wilder hopes of spring, lapped them round in an unexpected serenity.

On Monday morning Flecker and Browning made early visits to Somerset House and to the British Show Jumping Association, and then they fought their way out of London, through the heat and the dust and the traffic. At eleven thirty they emerged from the pine and rhododendron country and into the farmlands which surround Frailford. The farmhouse, standing foursquare in the September sun, seemed a place of idyllic peace after the turmoil of the overcrowded roads.

Charity Chesterfield was gardening; weeding the rose bed in a desultory fashion, her mind elsewhere. She wore a gardener's apron, a hessian affair with a huge pocket across the front, over her cotton dress. When she saw the detectives walking up the flagged path to the front door she put her tools in her trug and went to meet them.

'Good morning, we came to have a word with you,' said Flecker.

Charity looked at him and her eyes were full of quiet, dispassionate grief, the grief of someone who has faced the anguish of a situation in thought until he is ready to meet it in fact.

'Yes, come in,' she said, and dropping her trug and gloves on the doorstep she led the way.

They sat down in the pleasant, shabby sitting-room. Flecker produced his bundle of envelopes and looked straight at Charity. 'You have kept the fact that you and Miss Hemming are half-sisters a very closely guarded secret,' he said, 'because of Hugh.'

'Because of Hugh,' agreed Charity, sagging deeper into her chair.

'The likeness between you and your sister isn't obvious, but it's there,' Flecker told her. 'It bothered me from the first; I knew you resembled someone I'd seen. And there's an affinity about your Christian names which gave me a hint.'

Charity didn't speak. She sat gazing straight before her and her plain, square and normally good-natured face was set stiffly in lines of pain.

'Miss Hemming would have been in her early twenties,' Flecker went on thoughtfully. 'I imagine that she didn't want to be saddled with her indiscretion, while you and your husband had already given up hope of having a child; for you to adopt him would probably have seemed the ideal way out of a difficulty.'

'Yes.' Charity's voice was low and infinitely weary. 'It did seem a good idea at the time. Joy thought she didn't want him, but she was over-persuaded, I think. Our parents were elderly, very old-fashioned and absolutely horrified. They painted a very one-sided picture of what life was like for an unmarried woman with a child. It doesn't do to over-persuade people—'

'Was there any trouble before your half-sister came to work for Miss Thistleton?' asked Flecker.

'Not trouble exactly, no.'

'Did she consult you before taking the job?'

'No,' Charity shook her head.

'She waited until your husband was dead,' said Flecker looking at one of his envelopes. 'I suppose it was to be a sort of revenge; she was going to torture you with perpetual skating on thin ice.' Charity showed no inclination to speak so Flecker went on, 'Then there was this trouble between the Keswicks and Miss Thistleton began to talk of leaving her money to Hugh and Sarah. That must have brought everything, the pent-up jealousies of years and years, to a head.' He waited, looking at Charity, but still she didn't speak.

'T.T. mentioned her plans to the secretaries. I imagine that Miss Hemming told you. Had she decided to tell Hugh that she was his mother? Did she see herself enjoying a comfortable old age, living on her rich son? But you knew what was going on in Hugh's mind,' Flecker continued after a pause. 'His fantasies about his real parents; you knew what a terrible blow the truth would be to him. What did you do?'

Charity didn't answer; she supported her bowed head on her hand and a long silence fell.

Flecker broke it. Ignoring the revulsionary feelings that suddenly beset him, he said quietly, 'You knew about the linseed, you knew about the thermos of milk shake and you knew, as almost no one else did, that your half-sister frequently drank the milk shake. On Saturday you were close to the Thistleton horse-box all day; you had unlimited opportunity to add the poison to the thermos.'

Charity sat up and looked at him. There was an air of weary, of almost piteous dignity about her, but still she didn't speak.

'Don't you think you'd better tell me what happened?' suggested Flecker. 'I'm going to find out sooner or later.'

Charity shook her head. Flecker got to his feet. 'All right,' he said, 'but I'm afraid we shall come back.'

Leaving Charity slumped in her chair, the detectives let themselves out into the sunshine. In the car Flecker sat for a moment in preoccupied silence, then he sighed and said, 'We'll go to Whittam House, but there's no desperate hurry. I want a certain amount of telephoning to have taken place before we get there.'

Browning took a sideways glance at Flecker and then drove off in silence, wearing a funereal expression and proceeding at an almost funereal pace.

As they came in view of the Whittam House gates they saw a silver-grey Bentley turn out into the road ahead and disappear in the direction of Hamberley.

'Looks as though they've had a visitor,' observed Browning. Flecker didn't answer, he was still deep in thought, but his preoccupied mood vanished abruptly when he saw Molly Steer standing on the front doorstep and looking up the drive with an air of agitation about her. He was out of the car as it stopped. 'What's happened?' he asked.

Molly blinked and swallowed. 'Oh, it's Joy, Miss Hemming, I mean. It's dreadful; I mean I can't make it out, it's so awful, I mean what can have made her do it?'

'Someone telephoned?' suggested Flecker.

'Yes, that's right. I don't know who it was, but Joy seemed very angry. And then she just took it all, with me there in the room. That's what seems so funny, I mean so *bare-faced,* to do it there before my eyes. I began to tell her that it wasn't right, but she just pushed past me and rushed out—*so* unkind. And I didn't know she could drive, I mean, not properly.'

'What did she take?' asked Flecker, his voice tense with controlled impatience as he got back into the car.

'All the week's housekeeping money and the wages. You see, generally we go to the bank on Fridays, but last Friday—'

'And Miss Thistleton's car?' Flecker interrupted her.

'Yes, and she scratched it on the garage doorpost as she got it out; whatever would Miss Thistleton have said?'

'A grey Bentley?' asked Flecker.

'I don't know what kind it is, I mean I don't *know* about cars, but it is grey,' said Molly doubtfully.

'Did she say where she was going?' asked Flecker, as Browning put their car in motion.

'No, she just pushed past—' the rest of Molly's sentence was lost as they roared up the drive.

Flecker, recollecting his last conversation with Joy, remarked, 'She said she hadn't driven for "donkeys' years".'

'No licence then and no third party insurance,' observed Browning, swinging the car out into the road. 'Where do you reckon she's heading for?'

'London seems the obvious place,' answered Flecker.

'Difficult to do a disappearing act with a Bentley in the country lanes. Anyway we'll take a chance on it.'

They raced along the narrow road towards Hamberley, the car lurching protestingly as Browning held it firmly to its course and forced it on. They joined the main road and in a very few minutes approached the town. The lunchtime traffic was light but the streets were full of pedestrians: workers crossing the road to their regular cafés and restaurants, crowds of schoolchildren hurrying home to lunch.

'Come on, dear, that's right. No, you don't. Can't you see I'm in a hurry? Now Aunty, you wait a minute. Well really, some people ask for it!' monologised Browning as he hurried the car through the streams of recklessly inclined pedestrians.

Flecker said, 'I don't see any casualties being tended at the roadside, so it looks as though she got through all right, if she came this way.'

'I expect she got through just before one,' remarked Browning. 'Come on girls, I'm not going to wait about all night even if it is a pedestrian crossing. She'll have the legs of us on the open road.'

'I doubt it. If she hasn't driven the car before and she's out of practice, you'll catch her all right.'

They emerged from the congested streets and passed through a brief suburban district, then the road widened to carry three lanes of traffic; Browning began to build up speed. They came to the first roundabout, where they joined the new Upshott road, and then they raced on along the dual carriageway towards London. They were only about five miles from Hamberley when Flecker said, 'That looks hopeful; large grey Bentley ahead.'

Browning increased his speed, hooting to clear the offside lane before him he hurtled in pursuit.

Flecker said, 'I reckon it is her, she's putting on speed too.'

'Come on, get over,' Browning addressed two cars in the offside lane which were slowing his progress. He kept his hand on the horn until they reluctantly moved over and then with a grim look of concentration on his face he put his foot down again. There was only a long straight clear stretch between them and the Bentley and at once the gap began to narrow. They drew very near. Flecker made a note of the registration number and decided from the smallness of the figure driving that it must be Joy.

'We'll catch her on the next stretch,' said Browning, forced to slow up for an approaching roundabout. Joy didn't slacken her speed, the Bentley went away from them like a bullet. Too intent on the pursuit Joy hadn't noticed what lay ahead. As she came into the roundabout she braked violently and then suddenly lost control of the car. It hit the kerb surrounding the grass island, ricocheted across the road and crashed violently into a concrete lamp standard; there was a carnivorous crunch and the Bentley turned over, glissaded down the grass slope and came to rest with a rending sound on the wooden fence and hawthorn hedge below. It lay like a great beetle on its back, its wheels spinning slowly.

Flecker and Browning pulled into the side, jumped out and ran down the bank. The car doors were jammed. While Browning struggled with the least damaged and most accessible of them, Flecker took a look at the figure inside; at the twisted but curiously limp body, the yellowing whiteness of the drained face and the wounds which had scarcely bled. 'I don't think there's any desperate hurry,' he said.

The growing knot of people on the bank above began to offer advice. Someone ran to telephone ...

Joy Hemming was quite dead when they got her out. Flecker and Browning saw her body into an ambulance and explained matters to the local police officers who'd arrived on the scene; then they turned back.

'We'd better go straight to Frailford and break it to Mrs. Chesterfield,' said Flecker with a sigh. 'I imagine we shall get a statement from her now. Anyway,' he said more cheerfully, 'it's better for the boy. It's not much fun to have your mother doing fourteen years and we'd have had to drag the whole lot out at the trial.'

Browning said, 'It's after two so we've had the pubs, but Sergeant Dunster said that there was quite a nice little place along on the left here, where you can get a quick cup of tea and a sandwich.'

They told Charity Chesterfield of her sister's death and, though obviously grief-stricken, she remained composed and was able to make the long statement which Flecker needed. Then, after a short interview with Murray and Jackson in Hamberley, the detectives drove to Whittam House where Molly Steer received the news with less grief, but far more loss of composure. They spent about an hour in Joy Hemming's room and took several small objects with them when they returned to London.

On Friday the detectives drove down to Hamberley again, this time for the inquest and afterwards they spent some time at the County Police Headquarters indulging in tea and talk with Superintendent Jackson. It was nearly six when they drove up to Down End Farm and having parked the car in the yard beside the Land Rover, walked across to the house. Flecker had Theodora Thistleton's scrapbook under his arm, while Browning carried the double boiler. The white bull terrier welcomed them at the open front door and behind her, hearing their voices, came Laurence Keswick.

'Hullo,' he said, 'Scotland Yard; bearing gifts?'

Flecker grinned. 'Well, hardly gifts. Returning that which was loaned or lost.'

Marion Keswick joined them. She peered round her husband, who was blocking the doorway, to see what they were talking about; at the sight of the double boiler she flushed to a rosy pink. The three men looked at her.

Then Laurence said, 'My wife's been feeling very guilty about that wretched pot, but it was a more or less altruistic lie.'

'Yes, I know,' answered Flecker. 'At least I think I do.'

'Oh.' Marion looked at him. 'I knew that you didn't believe me; I lived in constant expectation of a heavy hand on my shoulder, but it never came; is that why?'

'I can explain that,' said Flecker, searching in his pockets. 'Where are my notes?'

'If we're going to go into this won't you come in and sit down,' suggested Keswick. 'Or better still, let's sit in the garden. And what about a drink? Are you permitted to hobnob now that the case is over?'

'Yes, we're off duty now,' Flecker told him, and Browning said, 'Just the job, sir. Inquests are thirsty work in this weather.'

'Oh now, it can't still be the inquest,' protested Flecker. 'Not after all the Superintendent's tea; you practically drank the County Constabulary's urn dry.'

'That tea wasn't made in an urn,' said Browning scathingly. 'The Superintendent has his freshly made in a pot.'

Laurence led the way across the lawn to where four very new garden chairs of various shapes and types stood round an equally new table. 'Acquired in an attempt to convince my wife that she really can sit down and leave everything to other people,' he said. 'Sit down, I'll just fetch the drinks.'

Marion sat down, looked rather apprehensively at the detectives and began to talk nervously about the garden. 'The lawn looks like a burnt offering,' she said. 'That always happens here if we get any decent weather. Laurence says that we've got to keep the house for at least another six weeks so that he can plant some trees for posterity. We've always longed to do it, but we could never afford to and I don't suppose anyone else who buys a place this size will be able to afford them either.'

'What are you thinking of planting, madam?' asked Browning.

'Oh, a mixed lot,' answered Marion. 'Two of everything that likes chalk—planted in positions where they will block out the worst of the view; and some fruit trees.'

Flecker said, 'It must have been a very pleasant view

once, before that lot,' he indicated the petrol stations and Sid's Café, 'arrived. And it's curious how much worse man's work looks in the country; you'd hardly notice them in a town.'

'It's the cars which haunt me,' Marion told him. 'All those expensive little objects rushing up and down all day; all that energy and petrol consumed and at the end of it so awfully little is accomplished.'

'I don't suppose the occupants of the cars feel that,' objected Flecker. 'The hedonists have probably enjoyed themselves, and if not they've survived another day, so there's still tomorrow. The materialists have done either the nation's business or their own and are a fraction nearer steadying the economy or making a fortune. The misers have added to their hoards and the religious are one step nearer to the characters for which they will finally have to account.'

'The way some of them drive they don't deserve to survive,' complained Browning as Laurence appeared and placed a tray of bottles and glasses on the table. When he had poured out and they were all sipping reflectively Laurence said, 'Now, where were we? You knew that Marion had thrown the double boiler away and you didn't accept her story that it leaked. I must say you'd make a very bad murderer, darling,' he added, turning to his wife. 'You ought to have made sure it *did* leak before throwing it away; a couple of minutes with a hammer and nail would have lent verisimilitude—'

Flecker had spread his envelopes on his knees. 'Oh yes,' he said, 'it was the rather banal fact that the dustbins are emptied on Mondays which more or less convinced me that Mrs. Keswick wasn't responsible for the crime.' He looked round at them. 'You see the murder itself was obviously premeditated and quite well-planned; it seemed to me that if that sort of murderer intended throwing the brewing apparatus into the dustbin she would have done it *before* committing the crime, in which case it would have been safely on the rural district rubbish tip. But if Mrs. Keswick had begun to suspect that her husband was involved, then she might try to conceal evidence after the crime was committed. I decided that most probably she hadn't connected linseed and hydrocyanic acid until late on Monday or perhaps even Tuesday and then she'd taken panic measures.'

Laurence Keswick was remembering with embarrassment his behaviour on the night the double boiler had been found.

'I was in a hellish temper the evening I caught you poking in the dustbin,' he said suddenly. 'I think it was the funeral; I'd come to and realised poor Theodora had been poisoned and had died, probably in agony. Before that I'd been wandering round in a euphoric daze feeling as though I'd just come up on the pools. But you didn't seem to suspect me particularly,' he went on. 'I couldn't understand it, I seemed the obvious person.'

'I did suspect you, in so far as I suspected everyone,' answered Flecker; 'one can suspect without being unpleasant or aggressive about it. But there were so many red herrings urgently awaiting investigation that I didn't have much time to spare for you. Also it seemed to me that you were rather involved at that show and I felt that you could hardly have poisoned the milk shake without an accomplice. If Mrs. Keswick was your accomplice then we were back at the foolishness over the double boiler.'

'I see,' said Laurence hastily, when he realised that Flecker was trying—out of tact—to avoid any mention of Helen Farrell. 'And I gather that you produced a terrific case against Charity, but she said that at the same time you seemed to cast doubt on it and she felt that you knew the real truth.'

Flecker looked through his envelopes. 'From the moment I knew that either Miss Hemming or Miss Thistleton might have drunk the milk shake Mrs. Chesterfield became less suspect as she would have had to risk getting the wrong person—and Miss Hemming and Miss Steer more suspect. Miss Steer, you see, would have poisoned the milk shake on its way to Miss Thistleton. The rest of you would imagine that only T.T. drank it and so your position was unchanged. Miss Hemming became the most suspect of everyone because Friday's drink remained untouched; possibly that was poisoned too. However, she didn't at first sight seem to have any particular motive; except that she might have had enough of the rather bullying treatment to which, I gather, all the staff were subjected. But gradually the vague likeness between Mrs. Chesterfield and Miss Hemming dawned on me and I was also struck by a certain affinity between their Christian names. Then Hugh's escapade came to light. He told me about his adoption and he also pointed out to me that he bore a slight resemblance to his adopted mother. After a visit to

Somerset House I found I could make a case against Mrs. Chesterfield for the attempted murder of her half-sister, but there were various points which made me doubt whether this was the right answer. First, the fact that she knew there was a risk of T.T. drinking the stuff and to risk that before the will was altered seemed to me madness. Then there was her behaviour; she seemed so very obviously afraid and if it was herself she was afraid for why was she thrown into such a state by Hugh's behaviour? And why when she had learned about the theft of the scrapbook was she still afraid?'

'Poor Charity, she has had a life,' said Marion sadly when Flecker paused. 'After Joy's death she told us about the row they'd had when Joy went over to tell her that T.T. was disinheriting Laurence and dividing the money between the children. She said that when Hugh was rich Charity couldn't expect her to keep quiet any longer and of course he'd want to support his mother. At first Charity just tried to persuade T.T. not to disinherit Laurence but when she refused to listen she had to tell her about Hugh and Joy.'

'I gather that my cousin was equally furious with all of them and accused Charity of trickery,' Laurence broke in. 'But later on she cooled down and decided to divide her money between Charity, Sarah and Marion.'

'Yes, and that must have been too much for Miss Hemming. That her sister should have money on top of marriage and both children was the last straw,' said Flecker. 'It was Cain and Abel again, hate and jealousy—the oldest and blackest of sins. Only Miss Hemming killed T.T. to prevent her sister from having the money and partly, I suspect, out of revenge for some very hard words. I gather that Mrs. Chesterfield had managed to persuade Miss Thistleton not to fire Miss Hemming out of hand, but she had it hanging over her and I understand from your solicitors,' he looked at Laurence, 'that any of T.T.'s employees who had been with her for more than a year at the time of her death will collect a couple of hundred pounds; that may possibly have hurried things up a bit.'

'What about those almonds in my mackintosh pocket?' asked Marion.

'That seems to have been just a stupid and malicious afterthought,' answered Flecker. 'We doubt whether she used almonds at all. When we came to look through her room we found, in the waste paper basket, an empty corn solvent bottle which smelt far more as though it had contained hydrocyanic acid than anything to do with corns. The wash basin also smelt as though it had recently received a stiff dose. Luckily she was in such a hurry to leave that she didn't rinse out the bottle and our lab was able to extract and identify one tiny drop. They tell us that it was pure acid and not mixed with an anonymous liquid as stuff brewed from almonds or linseed would have been. It's a Schedule One poison and she certainly hasn't signed a poison register under her own name but that doesn't mean very much.'

'What about Mrs. Pratt?' asked Laurence, refilling Flecker's glass. 'It's rumoured that you've put the B.S.J.A. on to her and she's down to appear before the Stewards.'

'It was Miss Thistleton,' Flecker explained, 'who found her out. The night before she was murdered T.T. sent for this scrapbook.' He opened it and turned the pages until he came to a group of four horses all wearing rosettes and a sturdy-looking duchess proffering a cup to the rider of the winner. The rider in second place was Christina Scott. Underneath, in neat block capitals, was a caption which read 'Cockchafer, second to Bay Buccaneer at Wembley', and below that, in T.T.'s sharply angular writing, had been added 'Top Ten?'

Flecker passed the book over to Laurence Keswick. 'You'll probably get there quicker than I did,' he said.

'I remember Bay Buccaneer well,' remarked Laurence, looking at the photograph. 'He won practically every class that year at Wembley, but they over-faced him or over-jumped him or something and he took to stopping. They brought him out again next year, but he wouldn't have it and when he'd jibbed all round the ring at Windsor, Gerry Luxton sold him as a hunter.' He looked at the photograph again. 'You mean Betty Pratt has got hold of him, hogged his mane, dealt with a couple of white socks and registered him as a Grade C horse; a nice new novice called Top Ten?'

'That's about it,' agreed Flecker, as Laurence handed the scrapbook to Marion. 'They've managed to trace the horse through half a dozen owners and it's definitely the one. Mrs. Pratt may be able to wriggle out by pleading ignorance, but I don't think she was ignorant. The fact that the horse went mysteriously lame on Saturday morning but made a complete recovery after T.T. died, doesn't sound like ignorance. What will she do now that I've deprived her of her rather shady living?'

'You needn't worry about that,' said Laurence

Keswick, getting up to refill Browning's glass. 'She has a boy friend who runs his own fish delivery business and I hear that if she's suspended he'll take over the ownership of the ponies and the little Pratts will jump as before. Top Ten, or rather Bay Buccaneer, won't be allowed to jump while he's suspended, of course, and afterwards he would have to return to Grade A classes, but still, he can always go back to hunting.'

'Well, perhaps we've taught Mrs. Pratt a lesson without much harm to her finances then,' said Flecker. 'I don't want to be haunted by three starving and spectral little Pratts.'

'I don't think Mrs. Pratt is capable of reform,' remarked Laurence. 'She'll just think the B.S.J.A. is being utterly unreasonable and when she's weathered the storm, she'll go back to her old ways.'

'I'm so sorry for the children,' said Marion sadly. Then she asked. 'What happened about Christina? You remember you said that I wasn't the only person telling lies?'

'Yes, very indiscreet of me,' answered Flecker. 'Well, I'm afraid that she's motivated entirely by demon pride, she can't bear to let anyone see what actually goes on inside her. It's not a criminal offence, but it must be a very uncomfortable state to be in. How is Hugh doing?' he inquired after a pause.

'You know that Charity told him everything?' asked Marion.

'She told me she was going to.'

'Poor Hugh, it was a terrible blow to him,' said Marion sadly. 'But one good thing has come out of it, his real father got in touch with Charity when he read about the case; he seems to have turned into rather a nice man and he's going to take an interest. No, two good things,' she corrected herself. 'Hugh is being much kinder to Charity, now he's stopped imagining that he belongs in top circles.'

'I'm glad to hear that,' said Flecker, 'for she seemed prepared to put up with an incredible amount for his sake.' He got to his feet and added, 'We must be on our way.'

'You're planning to move, I hear,' said Browning to Laurence Keswick as they walked towards the car.

'Yes, early next year I hope. I'm looking for a farm, something big enough to be economic, not like this place.'

'There'll be a drought,' objected Marion, 'and successive plagues of foot and mouth, fowl pest and swine fever. And all the crops will be struck with wilt and rust and blight. I hate farming, it's so depressing.'

'Now don't start that again,' answered Laurence, cheerfully unmoved. 'I've promised you your share in gilt-edged securities and solid-looking equities and I can't do more. If the farm goes bust you can say "I told you so" and dole me out a weekly allowance for the rest of my life and if there's a recession in the States and slump here at least the farm will feed us. I don't see how you can have greater security than that. Though, what with the bomb and lung cancer and the rapidly approaching indignities of old age, I really don't think money matters much, do you?' he asked, turning to the detectives.

'I suppose it gives one a warm and comfortable illusion of security,' answered Flecker, 'but perhaps that's a bad thing.'

And Browning said, 'A nice little bit behind you makes all the difference. I don't believe in living hand to mouth.'

They shook hands as they said goodbye and then the Keswicks stood close together, Laurence with an arm round Marion, waving until the police car was out of sight.

'Well, nice to see that all patched up, I must say,' observed Browning warmly. 'I never thought he'd do it, not when I saw Mrs. Farrell.'

Flecker, feeling suddenly sentimental, quoted,

' "Love comes back to his vacant dwelling, the old, old love we knew of yore" ', and then a sharp pang of unexpected jealousy made him wonder whether Lesley had written.

Also published by

Greyladies

GIN AND MURDER

by Josephine Pullein-Thompson

The pony book grows up!

In the villages of West Wintshire, deep in 'Horse and Hound' territory with their colonels, captains and brigadiers, a good-looking, rich and horsey young man keels over at a cocktail party and dies.

Local Inspector Hollis, a burly man with a low forehead, an aggressive nose, very little chin and an unfortunate manner, proves unequal to the challenge of finding the killer. Enter D.C.I. James Flecker of the Yard, whose amiable and unkempt appearance belies the fierce intelligence that suffers fools not at all.

Originally published in 1959.